A NEED SO BEAUTIFUL

SUZANNE YOUNG

BALZER+BRAY
An Imprint of HarperCollins*Publishers*

Balzer + Bray is an imprint of HarperCollins Publishers.

A Need So Beautiful
Copyright © 2011 by Suzanne Young

Library of Congress Cataloging-in-Publication Data
Young, Suzanne.
A Need so beautiful / Suzanne Young. — 1st ed.
    p. cm.
  Summary: A compelling Need that Charlotte has felt all her life is
growing stronger, forcing her to connect with people in crisis, but at
the same time other changes are taking place, and she is terrified by
what a doctor and family friend says must happen next.
  ISBN 978-0-06-200824-4
  [1. Supernatural—Fiction. 2. Dating (Social customs)—Fiction.
3. Best friends—Fiction. 4. Friendship—Fiction. 5. Foster home
care—Fiction. 6. Good and evil—Fiction. 7. Portland (Or.)—
Fiction.] I. Title.
PZ7.Y887Nee 2011   2010040810
[Fic]—dc22   CIP
                                                         AC

Typography by Sarah Hoy
11 12 13 14 15   LP/RRDB   10 9 8 7 6 5 4 3 2 1
❖
First Edition

For my grandmother Josephine Parzych,
who will never be forgotten

CHAPTER 1

I sit on the front steps of St. Vincent's Cathedral and pick at the moss nestled in the cracks of the concrete. I'm waiting for Sarah—as usual. She begged me all through calculus to go shopping with her, even though she knows I don't have the money for it. She promised it'd be fun. And she promised that *this* time she wouldn't be late picking me up. I rarely trust her promises, and yet I'm still here.

Traffic whizzes past the church and I look across the street to the bus stop. A thin woman is alone on the bench, a black umbrella open above her, blocking her face. But it's not raining. I glance up at the blue cloudless sky over Portland. The rainy season hasn't started yet. We have until November at least.

Just then a drop of water hits my hand. Then another

smacks my cheek. No way. When I look across the street again, the woman has moved to rest the umbrella on her shoulder. She's smiling at me, her blond hair spilling over her black jacket, her boots zipped high on her calf. She looks familiar. Something about her—

A bus pulls up to the stop, erasing her from my view. The sprinkles continue and I look back at the church, considering going inside for cover. The loud rumble of the bus pulling away startles me, and when I look it's gone and so is the woman.

And then the rain stops.

"Charlotte," Harlin whispers in my ear, and I jump. I hadn't heard him walk up.

I look sideways at my boyfriend as he straightens, grinning down at me. His unshaven chin and messy dark hair are a delicious contrast to me, sitting here in a plaid schoolgirl outfit with my fine, straight blond hair neatly combed.

"What are you doing here?" I ask, standing up. "Sudden urge to confess your sins?" Harlin lives on the other side of town with his older brothers. Six months ago he'd decided to drop out of St. Vincent's Academy, and although I'd hoped he'd enroll somewhere else, so far he hasn't.

"Nah," Harlin says. "Pretty sure you're the only thing that could get me this close to church again."

"I sound inspiring."

He laughs. "Well, that and I thought you might need a ride. Figured I'd swing by and check before heading to my mother's. I've been summoned for a *chat*." He looks away, clearly not wanting to talk about her. He never does.

I step closer and take his hand. "Well, I'm glad you're here."

He glances at me, his hazel eyes narrowing. "Is that right?" He pulls me into him and I get on my tiptoes, wrapping my arms around his neck. He leans down, his mouth barely grazing mine. "How glad?"

I smile, motioning toward the church. "Maybe not here?" Harlin shrugs and grins wickedly before kissing me again.

"You absolutely need confession," I whisper, and when he laughs, I take out my phone and check the time. "Sarah's nearly forty-five minutes late," I say, exhaling.

"You sound surprised. When in your life has Sarah ever been on time?" Harlin asks.

"Once last summer . . . Wait. Never mind. She sent her driver instead."

"I'm coming!" Sarah calls from around the corner. Before I even see her, I can hear the sound of her shoes clacking on the pavement until she finally appears near the street sign. She waves to me, gasping dramatically for air.

"And she arrives . . ." Harlin says, putting his arm over my shoulders. He turns and the scruff on his chin prickles my cheek. "Come to my house after?" he asks, his breath warm on my face.

"Mm-hmm." I close my eyes, loving the feeling of him so close. The security of his arm around me.

"Gross, you two," Sarah says, smoothing her red hair as she walks up. She's still in her uniform, although it's rolled at the

3

waist, the hem well above regulation length. She's switched out the usual black loafers for a scandalously high pair of spiked heels. Sarah likes to say that St. Vincent's dress code is only for the fashionably challenged. Maybe that's why my skirt is currently grazing my kneecap.

Unlike Sarah, I'm at St. Vincent's on a "tuition adjustment," which is code for I can't afford it. It's not like we're *that* poor, but when the yearly private school dues are enough to buy a BMW, it's a little tough to work into the family budget.

Truth be told, St. Vincent's is the best school in the state—even if half the people here are snobs. And that definitely includes Sarah. But at least she's my snob.

"Hey, Harlin," she says, glancing over at him. "You here for church, or will you spontaneously combust if you walk in?"

"Not today," he answers. "Seems they have a strict one-Antichrist-per-service rule, and you fill the quota."

"Ah, well. Guess I'll save a seat for you in the netherworld, then?"

Harlin grins. "Appreciate it."

Sarah turns to me, looking impatient. "Are you ready? I have ten zillion things to do before tonight."

I nod, sure that she's exaggerating. It's probably more like five zillion. Sarah's what the nuns like to call a "social butterfly"—not to be confused with a tramp. Which is what some of the other girls in our class like to call her. Of course, Sarah's family is richer than all of them combined, so they'd never say it to her face.

As the bells of the cathedral start to chime, I lean down to grab my backpack off the stairs. Suddenly I'm hit with heavy, bone-shaking vibrations that seem to run through my veins. They fill me up, take me over. Oh God. Not now.

"You okay?" Sarah's voice is far away, and when I turn to her, her eyes widen. "Again?"

Before I can answer, Harlin is next to me, pulling open my backpack. "Do you have your inhaler?"

I don't have asthma. It's just easier to pretend that I do. How else can I explain these episodes? No one would ever believe the truth.

Harlin shakes my inhaler and holds it to my lips. My eyes meet his, and he watches as I make a good show of taking the medicine even though the inhaler's empty.

The bells stop ringing and the humming inside me eases up, giving me time to catch my breath. My body is pulling me toward the cathedral doors, every inch of my skin aching to be inside. I don't know why. I never do. Not until I'm there. But right now I have to get inside that church.

Harlin puts the inhaler back into my bag, his jaw tight with concern.

"Thanks," I tell him, trying to sound calm. There are prickles of heat searing my skin. The throbbing will build slowly until I do what I'm supposed to. Resisting isn't an option.

"You scared me." Harlin looks away like he's over it, but I can tell he's still anxious. We've been through this before, but we both know that I'm getting worse. It's happening more often.

The Need.

I've been having these episodes since I was seven years old. An intense compulsion to go somewhere, see someone, do something. It's the most helpless feeling in the world, but I can't stop myself—like I have no choice. It used to happen only once a year, me telling a kid in my class not to steal, or stopping an old lady from taking the wrong medication. But then it became twice a year. Three times. Each Need becoming more intense. And lately, the compulsions have been coming on once a week. Sometimes once a day. But I've told no one. I'm not sure how.

"You use that inhaler way too much," Sarah says, shaking her head. "Can't you take a pill or something?"

"She tried," Harlin answers, not looking back at us.

It's not true. I've never taken any asthma medication, but I told him that to keep the cover believable. I don't want him to know about the Need. I don't want anyone to know. I'm still hoping it'll just go away on its own. But every day—with each Need—it looks more and more unlikely. I don't know what to do anymore.

On the wire stand next to the double doors of the church is the newsletter with today's service. I reach over and grab one, looking for a name. Anything that'll give me a clue.

"Um . . ." When I look up, Sarah's staring at me. "You're not going to ask me to go in there, are you? It's a funeral."

"It'll be quick, I swear." I wouldn't usually ask her to come, but I'm hoping if she's with me I'll be able to keep the Need

under control. Get in and out. Besides, if I leave her on the church steps now, she'll guilt me to death for ditching her.

I used to be able to pull off the Needs with minimum effort, but now they're harder to hide. Sarah's convinced herself that I'm partly clairvoyant, like a human Magic 8 Ball. All because she once saw me help a chaperone on a ninth-grade field trip find a lost hiker. She even thinks my visions trigger the asthma attacks.

I've considered that maybe I am psychic. But from everything I've read about them, they seem like scam artists. And sure, I see visions of people's future. But it's not just that. I can see their past. Their feelings. Their . . . souls.

Sometimes I go online at the library and check WebMD, plugging in my symptoms. But the closest diagnosis I get is OCD or schizophrenia. But I don't triple-check the locks and I don't hear voices in my head, so I'm resigned to the fact that I'm something else. I've even read all the booklets on saints in my religious instruction class, but I don't fit with them either. They knew their purpose. I wish I knew mine.

Sarah motions toward the church. "I'm not going."

"I'll be your best friend." I smile.

Sarah folds her arms over her chest, thinking about it. Under her makeup I can still see the hint of freckles across her nose. "Fine," she says. "But you're lucky that I hate everyone else or your little promises would be worthless."

"Thank you."

I look at Harlin and he's watching me, still concerned. He

knows nothing of the Need—what I really do when I leave him. And he's never asked. I think of it as a silent truce. I don't press him about his mother, and he doesn't press me about my unexplained disappearances. It works for us. At least for now.

"I'll see you soon?" I ask, reaching for him.

He gathers me up in his arms and puts his face against my neck. "Never soon enough."

I long for him. Then I wonder if anyone has ever felt the way I do about Harlin. Like I'm falling just from the sound of his voice. But at the same time I'm terrified, feeling that at any second he could be gone. That the Need will take me away from him.

"Let's go!" Sarah says, marching up to take me by the elbow. "The dead aren't getting any younger."

I turn and try to wave to Harlin but he's already down the gray stone steps on the way to his motorcycle. I still remember the first time I saw him at St. Vincent's Academy, the year before he dropped out. He was different from everyone else. He wore the same uniform, but something about the way he carried himself, he seemed so much calmer than the other guys. Peaceful. He was completely unforgettable.

"Harlin's looking good," Sarah says, stopping at the top step. "I like the whole rough-around-the-edges thing he's got going on. Makes him look dangerous."

"I like it too."

"I bet." She grins and adjusts the waist of her skirt, letting the hem down an inch or so. She glances at me and shrugs.

"What? I'm going into a church." Sarah reaches out to smooth down a strand of my hair. "Promise it'll be fast?"

"Superfast."

She exhales. "Fine. But first tell me, will I look hot tonight at the benefactors' dinner?"

"All signs point to yes."

"Thank you." She grabs the handle of the cathedral door. "You know this is completely weird, right? I have no idea why I enable your morbid gifts."

My shoulders tense. I feel exactly that way. Weird. Out of control.

"I don't know why you do either." I put my hand over hers and help pull open the door.

The sweet, smoky smell of incense immediately fills my nose and I close my eyes, taking it in. When I open them, I see the light filtering in from the huge stained-glass windows, casting colors on the mahogany coffin as it sits, lonely, in front of the altar. Father Peter is standing there, grasping the golden chain where the incense holder dangles, chanting and swinging the censer around the coffin where Stanley is surely resting.

I take Sarah by the elbow and move forward down the red carpeted aisle.

"This is humiliating," she whispers. "I want to sit in the back."

I pause, but find myself unable to turn away. I have to get closer to the altar, closer to the dead guy, Stanley Morris, and I let Sarah go.

Gaze focused on my black thrift-store Mary Janes, I step quietly toward the coffin. My mouth is dry, my skin feels hot all over—as if I'm sunburned.

A few people shift, creaking the wooden pews as I walk past, and I'm sure they're wondering who I am, and if I knew Stanley. I didn't. But I doubt I'm here for him—he's a bit beyond any help I could give him.

Suddenly, three rows from the front, a familiar rush of air moves through me. It doesn't ruffle my hair and I can't feel it on my face, but it's inside my body. I stop. I move to the pew on my left and look at the woman sitting there, her pregnant belly protruding. She presses her thin lips into a smile and scoots over, making room for me.

I nod thanks and sit. I look to where Stanley lies, his coffin closed. I wonder what he was like and what he would think if he could see all the people here now. It's sweet, really—how they all remember him and have come to honor his life. It's almost like he's not really gone. At least not to them.

"How did you know him?" the young blond mother asks me.

I look sideways at her, feeling dreamsick, nauseated. "I didn't, unfortunately. You?"

She glances at the casket, and then back at me. "Grandfather," she whispers. Her sadness fills me and I miss him too, as if I *am* her. I miss the time we spent at his cabin in Lake Tahoe, and the time he took me fishing in a canoe on the Colorado River. I miss the spicy smell of his pipe as he rocked on the

back porch of the house he'd built when I was a little girl.

I cover my face with my hands, startled and comforted by how cold my fingers are. I feel like I'm burning from the inside out.

"Are you okay?" the woman asks, touching my arm.

I turn to meet her red-rimmed green eyes. Her smooth, pale skin is graying slightly and I know why.

"When are you due?" I ask, her face getting hazy as light blots out the corners of my vision completely.

"Three weeks."

I squint, the radiance too bright. I'm trying to act normal so I don't scare her, but I know if I don't say it the Need won't go away. "Maureen," I whisper, unable to keep the words inside anymore. "The baby's not well. You need to see the doctor. You need to see him now."

Her face twists in both terror and anger, but I can tell that she knows; that maybe she's known for a while that something is wrong. She shakes her head at me, her voice rising slightly.

"What? How did you . . . who are you?" Her lips begin to tremble and I can see the familiar glazed look in her eyes. The same look they all get when the knowledge hits them.

I smile softly, the tension in my body fading, releasing me. She'll go, right now; she'll leave and go to the doctor. There's something wrong with her baby. And because I was here, she'll be okay. It makes me feel good.

"I'm sorry," I say, bowing my head. "I didn't mean to bother you." My body has returned to normal and I know I can walk away. There is no tug to be in this church anymore. I'm free.

I stand up and step out into the aisle. The pew creaks again and I can feel everyone watching me, probably confused and curious.

"Stanley was a good guy," I say quietly, motioning toward the coffin. I almost wince at my own words, but I don't know what else to say.

I'm halfway down the aisle, moving toward Sarah, who looks horrified, when I hear the padding of feet behind me.

"Excuse me," Maureen says, rushing past, not turning to me. She is out the door and into the sunlight by the time I reach Sarah. When I do, she shakes her head.

"'Stanley was a good guy'?" Sarah repeats, her right eyebrow raised. "Were you *trying* to look insane and unbalanced?"

I laugh and loop my arm through hers, my tense muscles all relaxed, leaving me almost euphoric. I flinch at a sudden burn on my shoulder, but it fades almost instantly.

"Let's go grab something to eat," I say, not looking back. "I'm starving."

CHAPTER 2

Sarah dips her fry in my ketchup—why? Not because I have the last ketchup packet on earth, but because she says the smell makes her gag. She can enjoy it only from a distance. And apparently two and a half feet across the table is enough for her.

I inhale the cheeseburger (no onions) that I ordered and gulp my diet soda. After a Need I find myself completely ravenous. I'm staring down at my plate, still thinking about the funeral, when Sarah says my name.

"What?" I answer, looking up at her.

"I asked if you had to go into the clinic tonight. God, I swear, you don't listen to a thing I say!"

It isn't true, but I can understand why she thinks that,

especially now. Our normally Sarah-centric friendship has been competing with my increasing Needs. When I disappear on nights we have movie plans or show up late for our shopping trips, Sarah thinks I'm blowing her off. But I can't tell her how often the Need hits, because if I did, she might rethink her clairvoyance theory. And I don't have a better one to offer.

"Of course I listen to you," I murmur, sipping from my drink.

"Then what did I say?"

I smile. "That you're the hottest thing to ever walk the halls of St. Vincent's and everyone wants you?"

"Close enough. Now, do you have to volunteer at the clinic tonight or not?"

"I was supposed to, but I asked for it off. Let me check." I take out my phone and dial up the office, waiting through the easy listening instrumental until the receptionist answers.

"Burnside Clinic," Rhonda says.

"It's Charlotte." I dip my fry in the ketchup. "Is Monroe around?" I eat while I wait for Monroe—Dr. Swift—to get on the phone.

"Tell Monroe I miss him." Sarah puckers her lips and makes a loud kissing noise. She likes to visit when I'm volunteering at the clinic, mainly to get a look at my boss.

Monroe Swift is barely over forty with slightly graying blond hair and a British accent. The Portland homeless community regards him as a saint. In fact, he's probably performing a tracheotomy with a ballpoint pen right at this very moment.

I personally find him brash and full of himself. Then again, he's been friends with my family so long it's like we're related.

"Yes, Charlotte?" Monroe's smart British accent rings through the phone. "What can we do for you?"

"Just checking to see how it's going tonight," I hint, hoping that if the waiting room is remotely calm, I might not have to go in.

I've been volunteering at the free clinic a couple nights a week for the past few years. I mostly enjoy it—filing papers, making copies—and I know it'll look good on a college application. At least that's what Monroe tells me. But now I just want more time for myself. Scratch that, more time for Harlin. There's never enough time for Harlin.

But instead of giving me time off, Monroe added shifts to my schedule. Instead of three nights a week, it's five. I've complained a few times but they pull the whole it's-for-a-good-cause card. Not. Fair.

More than anything, I just really hate working until ten. A free clinic in the middle of Portland doesn't exactly attract the best crowd when it's dark out. And yet, I can't imagine Monroe working anywhere else. He likes to play savior whenever possible.

I sigh. "Can I have today off or not? I asked you yesterday."

Monroe's silent for an excruciatingly long time. "I haven't had to perform CPR on the sidewalk out front, so it seems to be a slow night. Why, do you have plans?"

"Maybe."

"Well, then. Don't let the sick and incapacitated of Portland stop you. Run. Frolic."

"You're ridiculous."

"Why, thank you. To make it up to me you can come in tomorrow. Six sound good?"

"I knew there was a catch."

"Always is, sweetheart."

When I hang up, Sarah widens her brown eyes at me before popping a fry into her mouth. "Time off for good behavior? Monroe is feeling generous tonight."

"I have to go in tomorrow instead."

"He's a bastard." She pauses in her chewing. "So . . . I heard you and your boy toy whispering about sneaking around. Planning a sleepover, Charlotte?" She grins deviously. "And how will Mercy feel about this plan?"

Mercy Hernandez—my adoptive mother—splits her time between volunteering at a woman's shelter, working nights as an ER nurse, and raising foster kids as her own. Then again, with a name like Mercy, what else would she do?

"She's working at the hospital tonight." I smile, picking up my soda to bite on the straw before sipping. "And she doesn't get back until after school starts in the morning. And since I'm not going to the clinic tonight—"

"You're going to get naked. Yeah, I got it, Charlotte. Don't need the mental picture."

I nearly choke on my Diet Coke. Sarah has a habit of knocking everything down to the lowest common denominator, which to her usually involves getting naked.

"Will you drop me off at Harlin's place when we're done shopping?" I ask.

"Sure, but I have to go to Plato's. I need an outfit for this stupid benefactors' dinner out in Hillsboro. Do you think—"

"Yes, you'll look hot," I answer before she can finish asking.

Sarah's mother forces her to attend countless benefit concerts and dinners, all in the name of charity. They're all worthy causes; I just don't get the having to entertain people for them to give money. Why can't they just . . . give?

"Are you thinking self-righteous thoughts right now, Charlotte?" Sarah asks, a smirk pulling at her lips. "Not all saints are created equal, you know. Mercy does her thing physically, and my mother does hers socially."

It is a valid argument. Sarah's dragged me to a couple of events before, but they're like death to me. Stuffy people. Stuffy room. Sometimes I feel like her mother is watching me, as if being poor is contagious. It's like I'm a stray that Sarah brought home. I wonder if she's hoping someone else will adopt me soon.

My phone vibrates in my pocket and I pull it out to see a text message. Harlin.

Still with dead people?

I laugh and run my thumbs over the keys. *Worse. I'm sharing ketchup at Frankie's.*

"That Harlin?" Sarah asks, wiping her hands on a napkin and then tossing it onto the table. "Tell him I said to take a

17

cold shower. You'll be there later."

"Nice." Instead I type, *Sarah says hi.*

After a second Harlin's text pops up and I press my lips together and look across at Sarah. "Um, he says hi back."

"Yeah, right." Sarah starts piling the dirty plates on the tray and reaches over to take my soda out of my hand, shaking the ice around—confirming it's empty. She drops it on top of the tray and walks over to dump it all in the trash.

I watch after her when another text comes up.

I want you here now.

I cradle the phone in my hand, wishing I could kiss the screen and he'd feel it. It's tough with Harlin. I think I'd spend every second of every day with him if I could. He's like a want I can't describe. And I don't just mean physically. When I'm not with him, I feel almost empty. Lost. I can barely remember what it was like before him.

When Harlin transferred to St. Vincent's two years ago with scruffy hair and a leather jacket, it was like I'd been half-asleep for years and then suddenly woke up. Everything came into focus when I was with him. Sure, I had a few friends—I had Sarah. But something about Harlin—the way he looked at me. It was like I could suddenly breathe. He made me feel at peace.

Soon. I love you, I send back, and click my phone shut. I pause for a second, feeling the warmth fade from me, leaving me just a little bit lonely. After a long sigh I stand up and look around for Sarah. She's at the glass doors, her arm resting on the metal bar, staring at me.

For as long as I've known her, Sarah's been searching for *the guy*, the one who'll be good to her. Of course he also has to be hot, rich, funny, sensitive, masculine—but not macho—and want to move out of state after she graduates. With those requirements she's been looking for a while. Even if it's gotten her a not entirely deserved reputation.

Sarah knows how I feel about Harlin. Even if we seem a little intense at times, she knows he's my *guy*, so she doesn't complain. We're too drama-free and a little boring for her taste, but I'm pretty sure Sarah approves. She's a romantic like that.

"Red or black?" Sarah asks, a dress in each hand as she poses in front of the mirror. Of the eight that she's tried on, she's narrowed it down to these two dresses. She holds the black one up to her, tilting her head.

We're in Plato's, a hipster secondhand store that has the best selection of used clothing in Portland. Even though Sarah could afford to shop anywhere, she prefers this place. She says the clothes have more personality because people have lived in them. Squinting, she switches to the red dress.

I shrug. "Red is sexier, but the black makes you look smarter."

"Red it is." Sarah tosses the black dress across the patterned lounge chair and folds the red one over her arm, turning toward the front of the store. "I have some fabulous Jimmy

Choos at home to match this." She pauses to look me over. "Do you want to shop for something? I have my mom's charge card."

I shake my head as I lean against the wall. To be honest, I'm tired. Drained, really. Even if I do like the lime green coat on the mannequin in the front window, I don't have the energy to ask about it. Sarah likes to say that buying me stuff is payback for being her personal shopper. She doesn't buy a thing, not one stitch of clothing, until I've seen it and commented. Not that she takes my advice. She just likes the second opinion.

I walk with her toward the register. She looks sideways at me, biting her lip. "You know who's going to be at the dinner tonight?" she asks, as if I wouldn't know. Like every high school, St. Vincent's has an interesting mix of jocks, nerds, and everything in between. But there's only one guy right now who fills at least half of Sarah's requirements—Seth Reynolds. Seth is the captain of the swim team, and not nearly as obnoxious as his meathead friends. He and Sarah have had the whole flirty-eyes thing going for weeks, so I have high hopes for them. I know Sarah does too.

"Who?" I say anyway, feigning ignorance. I eye the coat in the window as we wait at the register.

"Seth! He's going with his parents. Isn't that so sweet?"

"Uh, maybe. Or maybe his parents force him to give to charity too."

"Oh, shut up," she says. "Anyway, I think he might ask me out tonight. Especially if I'm wearing this." She holds up the red dress. "What do you think? Can you see anything about tonight?"

I sigh. "Sarah, I have no idea. I'm not really psychic."

She waves me off and lays the dress across the counter. "Sure you are."

The dark-haired cashier with an arm full of tattoos and a barbell through her lip tilts her head like she's judging the garment. "This is hot," she says, before she starts to ring it up.

Sarah smiles. "Yeah? Thanks."

I feel a prickle of warmth across my cheek and I reach up to touch it. My heart slowly starts to speed up. No. It's too soon.

"I'm wearing it to some lame dinner," Sarah tells the cashier, but her voice is fading. "Do you think . . ."

I clench my teeth as my bones begin to heat up. Without completely freaking out, I touch Sarah's arm. I can feel sweat gathering at my temple.

"I'll meet you outside, okay?" I say, hoping it comes out right.

She glances quickly at me, nods, and then goes back to talking to the cashier. I see her mouth move, but I can't hear her. I hear my heartbeat.

My legs shift, but it's like they're not mine. They're taking me to the front of the store, to the window. I'm on fire now, especially my shoulder, and my head, it's like it's slowly imploding. As I pass the green coat a rush of wind blows through me. I stop.

The coat? I don't see how . . . but I pause. Behind it is a flyer taped to the window, facing the street. I need to pull the flyer off the glass, but I don't want to. I want to see Harlin. And if I get my next Need I'll have to go wherever it leads me. I don't have a choice.

My fingers shoot forward without my permission and pluck the paper from the glass, breaking the tape. Glancing at Sarah, I see her bent over as she signs her receipt.

With the flyer in my hands, I look down, seeing the image of the front bleed through the back of the white copy paper, but I don't want to turn it over. I don't want to have to go anywhere, yet I flip it to the other side.

Greens and blues splash across the page as I try to make sense of the words. But I can only read the address: 5918 W. Broadway. I blink quickly trying to read the rest, but it's impossible. All I can see is 5918 W. Broadway.

"Ready?" Sarah asks from behind me and I jump, the paper slipping from my hands. It zigzags through the air until it comes to rest just inside the platform of the window.

My muscles release. My body exhales.

"You okay?" Sarah takes my elbow and turns me to her. Her eyes are filled with worry and when she starts looking around, I tell her that I'm fine.

She gasps and I wonder if she can tell—tell that the Need has returned and I can't stop it. She meets my eyes accusingly and I step back from her.

"Liar!" she says. She stomps past me and for a second I think she's going to grab up the flyer, but she doesn't. She practically rips the coat off the mannequin and holds it up admiringly.

"You want this!" she says. "And here you are drooling over it. How many times do I have to tell you, if I didn't want to spend money on you, I wouldn't? God, you're so humble you make me want to vomit."

She laughs and holds up the coat, looking toward the registers. "Raven?" she calls sweetly. "Can you add this on the charge?"

I don't look back but I assume the cashier agrees because suddenly Sarah is wrapping a lime green jacket over my shoulders. My fingers have almost stopped shaking and I feel close to normal. Not as good as when I left the funeral, but this is bearable. It's like a nagging feeling; something you have to do when you don't want to. But I know that even if I try to resist, I can't. I've never been able to before.

Facing Sarah, I slip my arms into the coat.

"Do you think Harlin will like it?" I ask, tying the waist.

Sarah nods her approval. "Absolutely. Oh." She claps her hands together. "You should totally show up at his house wearing this." She smiles. "And *only* this."

"Tempting," I say. "But I think I'll save that genius plan for when we're living together." After next year, Harlin's going to move out of his brothers' place and we're going to rent a one- bedroom apartment in the Pearl District, something small but charming. I'll be attending Portland State—even though I have no idea what to study. I'm hoping a major will come to me eventually, but so far, it hasn't. My future is a blank slate, full of possibilities.

I haven't told Mercy about our plans, but I'm sure she'll approve. Or at least I hope she will.

"Aw," Sarah coos sarcastically. "You two will be so cute playing house. Maybe you can adopt dogs to pose as children too. Dress them up in little sweaters."

"Oh my God, shut up."

"Harlin can go work at some filthy garage, fixing motorcycles, and then he'll come home all dirty. And you'll be there—his little woman—cooking dinner while wearing this jacket. With nothing underneath."

"Wow." I laugh. "That's a bright future you have planned for us."

"I'm part clairvoyant, too."

"You're also part moron." I grin at her as we walk outside, the noise of traffic immediately assaulting our ears. I don't mind the sounds, though. At least right now my hearing isn't plugged by the Need.

Sarah hooks my arm and bumps her shoulder into mine. "I'm just kidding about the playing-house stuff. I know you're going to be great at whatever you do," she says, sounding suddenly sentimental.

I look at her. "So will you."

She crinkles her nose. "Don't think my father would agree with that."

I don't respond. Daddy conversations are something that Sarah usually reserves for alcohol-induced moments. She glances away just as the sun pokes out from the clouds, only staying for a second before fading behind the tall buildings.

"Anyways," she says with a heavy sigh. "Let's get back to talking about Harlin and how he'd want you to show up naked under this jacket."

I shake my head. "I think I know what Harlin wants."

"Hmm . . ." Sarah says, flipping her hair over her shoulder. "I bet you do." She snorts and our shoes beat a steady rhythm on the concrete as we head to the garage where her father's Beamer is parked. Sarah's been driving her father's car since we were fifteen—unless you count that time when we were twelve and skipped out on gym class to grab a milk shake at Frankie's. She nailed a trash can while trying to park and then spent two hundred dollars of her allowance getting it fixed before her father found out.

Sadness washes over me. That was before the Need took over, back when I only had to sneak away once, maybe twice a month. That was when I had more time.

Sarah clicks open the locks of the car, and as I climb in I start to work on my exit strategy to get to Harlin's. First I'll check in with Mercy and pretend to settle in for the night. Once she's gone, I'll slip out.

Sarah starts the car and drives out of the garage, talking about how she's sure Seth has been staring at her in physics class. But it's hard to listen. There's an image that I can't shake. And I know it won't stop until I get there: 5918 W. Broadway.

CHAPTER 3

As I push open the heavy wood door to my fifth-floor walk-up apartment, Mercy is there—her black hair knotted tight near her neck, her pale blue scrubs crisp from too much starch.

"And where were you?" she asks in her thick Puerto Rican accent. Even though she sounds brusque, I know she's just being protective. Sometimes that involves dragging Alex out of a rave on a Friday night, or picking me up at Harlin's when I'm there too late. But recently her schedule at the ER became more demanding, giving us opportunities to sneak out. Not that we take advantage of it. Much.

I drop my backpack on the floor by the couch and untie the belt of my jacket. "Sorry. Sarah had to get a dress for some

fancy dinner she's going to tonight."

"You can't call me?" She pauses and touches the green sleeve of my coat. "This is lovely, by the way."

"Thanks. And you're right, I should have called. I will next time."

"Mm-hmm," she huffs. "And I'm assuming you're in for the night now that you've gotten Sarah's shopping out of the way?" She's not hinting. She's telling me.

"Of course."

"Good. You know I don't like you riding the bus when it gets late. I told Alex that too, but I know his little fifteen-year-old butt was out after twelve." She raises her voice so that it carries toward his bedroom. "He's lucky he's not grounded."

I smile, knowing that Mercy would never ground us. Scold us endlessly, yes. But never punish us. It just isn't her way.

I've been with Mercy for over ten years, longer than Alex or Georgia. She used to tell me about the day she first saw me in the hospital, a six-year-old with a pale pink dress and ribbons in my hair, sitting all alone in the waiting room. No one knew who dropped me off, or whom I belonged to.

Mercy had just gotten her license to foster, so when no one claimed me, she put in a request to take me home with her. After nearly a year of searching, my parents were never found, so Mercy filed to become my legal guardian. She likes to say that *I* found *her*.

It used to haunt me, not having natural parents. I've tried so many times to remember my early childhood, but nothing

27

comes to me. Like I didn't exist until the moment I sat down in the hospital waiting room. Mercy and Monroe both think my memory loss is post-traumatic stress. They say it sometimes erases painful experiences.

But I gave up dwelling about my past a long time ago. There's no reason to. Mercy treats me like her own, and with Alex here with us, it's like we're a real family. We've each found the place where we belong.

I've never told them about the Need. As far as Mercy knows, I have terrible menstrual cramps and severe asthma. The Need usually knocks the air out of me, so it wasn't really hard to fake not being able to breathe. When I was a kid, I was too scared to ever tell Mercy about my episodes, afraid that if she found out she'd realize I wasn't normal, and then she'd give me back.

And now it's been so long that I'm not sure how to bring it up. I don't know, maybe I'm still scared of losing my only home.

A door closes and Alex comes from the hall, his toothbrush sticking out of his mouth as he runs his hand through his still-wet, shoulder-length black hair. When he sees me, he waves.

"Hey, Charlotte," he mumbles through clenched teeth. "Nice coat."

"Thanks. Going out?"

Alex takes the toothbrush out of his mouth. "Nope. Staying in. You?"

"All night."

We smile at each other and I slip off my jacket, laying it over the back of the tweed sofa. Like me, Alex sneaks out to see his boyfriend during the week. It's just so much easier than asking for permission, which we'd never get.

Mercy mumbles something in Spanish to Alex as she walks past him into the kitchen, obviously still mad about his late-night bus ride. He rolls his eyes at me while Mercy takes a Tupperware filled with leftovers from the fridge.

The house is quiet, and I wonder why loud rap music isn't coming from the back bedroom as usual. "Hey," I ask Alex. "Where's Georgia?"

"Hell if I care," he says, shrugging and sitting on the stool at the counter.

Mercy walks by and lightly smacks him in the back of the head. "Be nice to your sister."

I laugh because Georgia and Alex fight like actual brother and sister, even though Georgia has only been here about six months. She's totally secretive and often bitchy, but then again, most fosters who come through start off like that. Alex and I were the only ones who became permanent. Neither of us ever had anywhere else to go.

"She's not my sister, Ma," Alex replies. "Not unless you're going to adopt her, too."

"Georgia has a family down south," Mercy says, putting the Tupperware in her insulated lunch bag. "And if it weren't a temporary situation, maybe I would." She raises her chin defiantly and I can see in her eyes that she feels guilty. Sometimes I think that Mercy would adopt the whole world if she could.

"Charlotte," Alex says. "Back me up here. Georgia sucks, right?"

I laugh. "I'm not saying a word."

"Good girl," Mercy calls out as she crosses the room to pause in front of me, purse and lunch bag in her hands. "I have to go," she says, sounding disappointed. "I'm sorry, I know I said I'd try to be around more."

"It's okay." And it is, because if Mercy were around more I'd have fewer chances to sneak out and see Harlin. "Maybe this weekend?"

"We're going to church on Sunday," she says like it's a warning. "Sister Catherine has been all over me about missing Mass." As a family we consider ourselves part-time Catholics. We reserve church for holidays, baptisms, and funerals. It's not that we aren't religious; we just prefer to say our prayers before bed instead of in a cathedral full of people. But every so often one of the nuns at St. Vincent's reminds Mercy that a scholarship is a "gift from God" and that we should give back by attending Mass. Basically they guilt us into going.

"Charlotte," Mercy says, "are you feeling okay? You look sort of pale." She reaches out to touch my forehead.

I nod, but now that she mentions it, anxiety begins to turn in my stomach. I'm resisting the Need by waiting, but I have to, even if it makes me a little sick. There's not a lot of time and I still want to see Harlin.

"I'm just tired," I say.

Mercy purses her red lips, lines of worry creasing her

forehead. "You call me if you feel sick tonight. Monroe told me your asthma attacks have been kicking up." Mercy and Monroe have been friends for years, ever since she brought me to his clinic when I was seven with a broken arm. And luckily Monroe buys my asthma story, at least for now. If he didn't keep Mercy updated on it, I'm not sure my acting skills would be enough for Mercy to keep believing the story. How many asthma attacks can one person have?

"I'll be fine," I say.

"Good. Now go rest." She leans forward to kiss the top of my head. "I'll see you after school. Tomorrow we're having a family dinner. Tell Georgia if you see her."

"Su-ucks," Alex sings from the kitchen, but we both ignore him.

"I'll tell her," I say to Mercy. "Night." I turn to walk toward my small bedroom in the back of the apartment, but stop in the hallway to wait. The minute I hear the click of the front door shutting, I smile and go to change out of my uniform.

"Looking snazzy, Miss Cassidy," Harlin says when he opens his apartment door. His vintage T-shirt and loose jeans hang on him just right, and his hair is messy in that I-don't-care sort of way. As he smiles, his dimples deepen and I get butterflies all over, like I always do when he's watching me like that. Like he wants me.

"Thank you," I say, holding his stare, tingles racing up and down my body.

Harlin bites his bottom lip as he looks me over. "Where'd you get the jacket? It's hot."

"Sarah." I spin around slowly, showing it off. "Cute, right?"

"So cute. Now come here." He reaches out, putting his hands on either side of my hips to pull me toward him. When we're against each other, he pauses just as his lips touch mine. "Don't kill me," he whispers, "but my brothers are home."

Disappointment fills me, and I pout a little, moving back from him. "Both of them?"

"Yep."

I sigh. Harlin's brothers are both in their twenties, and even though they're pretty cool, they aren't exactly fine with us spending the entire time in Harlin's bedroom. I glance around the empty hallway of his apartment building. Well, at least out here we're alone.

I push him hard against the yellowed wall before pressing my mouth to his. He reacts immediately, pulling me into him, against him. I reach up and tangle my fingers in his hair. He tastes like cinnamon, just like always. Just like he did that first time he kissed me nearly two years ago.

Before then we'd never spoken, only saw each other in the halls of St. Vincent's. I would watch him, half-fascinated, half-intimidated. Because while all the other guys were acting like idiots—punching one another in the halls, pinching girl's asses—Harlin kept to himself, always seeming lost in his thoughts. But when he looked at me, I got a rush. I felt alive.

Then Portland had this huge winter storm, the entire city

blanketed in ice and snow. And when the power in the school went out, I found myself in the hallway of St. Vincent's, rushing to class from the bathroom. The old hallways were dark and creepy. The usual humming of the lights silent. Dead.

I was nearly back to economics class when I felt someone touch my arm as I passed the art rooms. I spun, startled, and saw him. Green paint was smeared across his hands and now on the white sleeve of my shirt. When I looked into his hazel eyes, my heart started beating wildly, as if electricity was coursing through me.

Neither of us spoke as we watched the other. But in that moment I took in a long breath and it felt like my lungs were filling for the first time. As if I'd never truly breathed before.

Across from me Harlin shook his head quickly, his dark hair falling in his eyes. "Sorry," he said, reaching for my hand. "I just wanted to meet you. I'm Harlin." His voice was soft and raspy and I realized that it was the first time I'd heard him speak.

"Charlotte Cassidy," I answered, letting him take my hand. But he didn't shake it. He just held it.

His mouth twitched with a smile and his dimples deepened. "Where were you running to, Miss Cassidy?"

My stomach fluttered as I stood there, forgetting where I was going. Where I was supposed to be. Instead, like it wasn't even my choice, I moved forward to stand incredibly close to him.

"I was running here," I said, sounding confident. I'd never

wanted to talk to any other guy before. Not like this.

Harlin looked me over, and then he dropped my hand to put his palms on either side of my face before leaning down to press his lips to mine. Barely touching me at all.

He tasted like cinnamon.

Just like he does now, pulling me against him in his apartment hallway and keeping me close. "Missed you," he murmurs between my lips, still kissing me.

And I take what I can, every minute I can. Because I know that tonight there's somewhere else I have to be.

"Hey, Charlotte," Harlin's brother Jeremy calls from the living room when we finally make it into the apartment. He's sitting on the cracked leather sofa, watching ESPN in his pajama bottoms.

"I see today is business casual?" I motion toward his pants as I set my coat on the dining table.

"Only the best for you."

I laugh and look around the place. Sneakers are piled near the door and last night's pizza box is still on the kitchen counter. Three guys living in a two-bedroom apartment can get kind of cramped. Especially when I'm here.

But on the nights when both of Harlin's brothers are at work, we just lie shoulder to shoulder on his bed, talking about our future. How our apartment in the Pearl District will have a spot for a studio so Harlin can paint. How I'm hoping to figure out what I want to do once I'm at Portland State. And most of all, we talk about how we'll take a trip to California because it's where he grew up. It was a time when he had his dad. On those nights Harlin promises to take me everywhere.

The other nights we just watch *SportsCenter*.

Jeremy slides over, making room for me on the couch. I drop down next to him and the anxiety begins. It feels like little vines are twisting in my stomach, making their way through my body, trying to pull me out to the street. I swallow hard and resist.

"Charlotte, you want a soda?" Harlin asks from the kitchen. I turn toward him, my head feeling heavy.

"Please," I answer.

Jeremy picks up the remote and starts clicking through the stations. "So Charlotte, you still planning on Portland State?"

"Yep." I can feel sweat beginning to gather above my lip as Jeremy looks over at me.

"Good girl." He lowers his voice, glancing toward the kitchen. "You know he's been studying for his GED, right?"

I smile. "I know."

Jeremy nods to himself and goes back to flipping through the stations. "You're a positive influence on him," he says. Then louder, "No idea how an idiot like him got a girl like you."

"Bite me, Jeremy," Harlin says with a laugh as he comes back into the room, holding two cans of soda—one diet and one regular. I take the diet soda thankfully because anxiety is making my mouth dry. I just want to stay here. I don't want to leave yet.

"Where's Henry?" I ask Jeremy. Henry is the oldest brother—nearly twenty-seven. He looks a lot like Harlin, only taller and with blue eyes. But Henry is the muscle around here. He works long hours and sets the rules. I sometimes wonder where Harlin would be without him. If he'd be on the street somewhere, anywhere to be away from his mother.

Jeremy smacks the back of the remote to get it working again, and then points it at the TV. "Henry's in his room, on the phone."

"Girl from the restaurant?" Harlin asks.

"No. Mom," Jeremy says quietly, looking over. Harlin shifts next to me, but doesn't say anything. I lower my eyes and stare into my lap.

When Harlin was sixteen, his father—a policeman—was killed on duty. It was shortly after they'd moved to Oregon, and his dad had been overseeing a drug bust at an abandoned house on the west side. Then someone pulled out a gun and shot him. He bled to death before the ambulance arrived, and the shooter was never found.

Harlin doesn't like to talk about it, but his mother does. All the time. She thinks by reliving it over and over that she's paying homage or something. She even built a shrine to him in her bedroom. It's completely unhealthy.

But Harlin, he's never dealt with his grief. Last year he started falling behind in his classes, getting in trouble for skipping. He completely withdrew. Everyone thought he was a slacker, but I knew he just missed his dad. And his mother was making it worse by not letting him forget, calling all the time, begging him to move back in. Eventually Harlin just dropped out of St. Vincent's and got a job working at a garage on Alder Street a few afternoons a week. But now he's studying for his GED and I think it's kind of awesome. He's kind of awesome.

When the apartment stays silent too long, Jeremy exhales and puts the TV back on ESPN. Just then Henry stalks out of the bedroom, phone still in his hand.

"Hey," he says to us, pushing Harlin playfully on the side of the head. "Mom says to call her later."

"Okay," he answers, taking his arm from around me. But I know he won't.

"You'd better," Henry says. "Hi, Charlotte," he adds before turning around.

Jeremy sets the remote on the coffee table and stands up to stretch. "I'm going to run and pick up some Chinese food. You guys want?"

I shake my head, knowing I won't be able to stay long. My temples are already starting to throb.

"Yeah," Harlin says, fishing in his jeans pocket and pulling out a ten. He gives his order and I stare at the TV, not really able to hear it. My ears are plugged. I'm running out of time, but I don't want Harlin to notice. I want to be with him.

Jeremy takes the money and heads toward the back bedroom to get dressed.

"Chinese? I'll come with," Henry calls, but then pauses to

look at us, one eyebrow raised.

Harlin laughs and puts his arm around me. "Don't even say it," he warns. "You'll embarrass her." But he always says it.

"Charlotte," Henry begins in a mock parental tone, "when two people love each other, they may have certain urges. Protection is an important—"

"Oh my God!" I cover my ears and laugh. I wait until his lips have stopped moving before I drop my arms.

"Now, behave," he adds, glaring at us before leaving to go down the hall.

Even though both Henry and Jeremy have given us *the talk*, they act like we're a couple of uncontrollable animals. It's humiliating.

The minute Henry's gone, Harlin pulls me to him so he can whisper in my ear. "I didn't think they'd ever leave."

I smile. "Me either."

Harlin eases across the bed, resting his face close to mine before he kisses me. His soft, full lips fit to mine perfectly, and he pauses before kissing me again.

I love him.

His hand slips past my ear and into my hair, drawing me closer. He turns on his back, rolling me on top of him and we kiss. I don't ever want to not be with him, because when I am, I feel normal. I sit up and look down at him, my hands resting on his chest.

"So beautiful," he murmurs, reaching to unbutton the silver

tabs of my shirt. "You're so damn beautiful." His eyes are searching me as he slides the fabric off my shoulder and sits up to kiss the skin there.

Heat is pulsating through me. I don't want him to stop. I don't want—

"Baby?" he says, touching my shoulder gingerly. "What happened?"

"What?" I ask, my voice raspy. "What's wrong?" My head is spinning from desire and for a second, I'm still swaying. I look sideways over to where his finger is gently rubbing. It's the same spot that hurt earlier in the church.

"Looks like a burn," he murmurs, adjusting his position so that he can sit up and examine it better.

When Harlin moves his hand, I can finally see the patch of skin—red, slightly raised. It's about the size of a quarter, but it looks like it should really hurt. Only it doesn't. At least, right now it doesn't.

Harlin touches my chin and turns me to him. "Did something happen?" His hazel eyes are wide with protectiveness. I shake my head and press my lips together to assure him.

"I must have hit it on something," I say, somehow knowing it's not true. "Maybe at Plato's."

Harlin's face softens as he balances me on his thighs, facing him. "You gotta be more careful," he whispers, leaning forward to kiss the spot. "You know it makes me a murderous psycho to think of you getting hurt."

I laugh. He's exaggerating. The closest he's ever come to

murderous psycho was the time he told Mercy's old landlord to drop dead for locking us out. But other than that, he's even-tempered. Harlin is a gentle soul. Always has been.

His mouth touches my neck, and I put my hands in his hair, blinking slowly. But as soon as I close my eyes, feeling Harlin's hand sliding to my waist, I see it. It's all I can see: 5918 W. Broadway.

I straighten, trying to heave in a breath, but it feels caught. I wheeze and Harlin takes me by the upper arms and moves me over on the bed.

"Charlotte," he says loudly, putting a hand on my cheek. "Are you having an attack?"

Not now! Not now! But I shake my head yes, making high-pitched noises as I touch at my chest, trying to stay calm. I knew this would happen. I waited too long.

"I'll be right back," he says, scrambling off the bed. "Stay here." He moves quickly toward the bathroom down the hall. Harlin makes me keep an inhaler in his medicine cabinet. I have one at Sarah's, too. But I can feel that my cover story is beginning to wear thin. Who has asthma like this?

My body is convulsing, lurching forward with each gasp. I should be there by now. I'm late. When I wait too long, the Need gets more powerful. More . . . painful.

The minute I hear Harlin's bare feet on the wood in the hallway, I clutch my shirt closed and climb off his bed, slipping my feet into my shoes. My head is beating a steady pace with my heart and I wish I could just stay here, in Harlin's room.

But I know I can't. This won't stop until I do what I have to—whatever is needed at 5918 W. Broadway. I stare out into the hallway, hearing Harlin open the medicine cabinet.

Turning away, I stumble toward his bedroom window, gripping the frame. Pushing it up takes nearly all of the strength I have left, but it's the only way out. I can't risk walking past the bathroom and having him stop me.

I put one leg at a time over the sill and step out onto the steel grid of the fire escape. I snake my body through the window until I'm out in the dark night, standing above an alleyway. I quickly move down the stairs, buttoning my shirt as I go. I pause once to feel the odd patch of skin on my shoulder, but I'll have to look it over later. When I'm done.

My breathing improves now that I'm moving. My bones begin to warm a little. Just enough to tell me that I'm going the right way.

CHAPTER 4

It's nearly twenty blocks later when I'm standing in front of a crumbling old warehouse, the number 5918 painted on the red bricks. The broken panes of glass are jagged like sets of sinister teeth. This is a really bad idea. There is no way in hell I'd be out here if it wasn't for the Need. This side of Portland isn't the safest place to be at night.

A wave pushes through me and I stumble toward the over-sized metal doors. A flyer—the same one from Plato's—is taped in the window. Next week there will be a community event to restore the building, something truly inspiring, I'm sure. But tonight it's still just an abandoned warehouse. And a creepy one at that.

I step back. Need or not, there is no way I'm going inside.

Chances are, there could be a junkie or dealer living inside. It wouldn't be the first time the Need has put me in this position. Last month I walked into the dark back room of a restaurant. It was filled with drug dealers, their guns out on the tables. I told Anthony that his girlfriend was pregnant and needed him to straighten up. That if he didn't, she'd leave and he'd never see his kid. I thought for sure I was going to get killed that night, but instead, he listened. And I walked out unscathed.

But that doesn't mean I wasn't scared. No . . . whatever it is I'm here for now, I can do it from outside. At least there are streetlights.

There's an intense heat running under my skin, setting my shoulder on fire. I move the white fabric of my shirt to peek at it. The red blotch is darker now in the center. I feel my stomach turn at the sight. It wasn't like this at Harlin's.

I touch it because warmth is pulsating down my arm, seemingly from that spot. But as I brush the skin . . . it rubs off. I hitch in a breath, my eyes wide. I wipe my finger softly over the raised area again and another layer comes off. It's like goldleaf on a cheap antique—just flaking away.

I'm starting to hyperventilate, but the pain seems to fade with each swipe I take. I press a little harder as I run my fingers over the spot and soon there's no more skin there. I cry out at the sight of it and cover my eyes with my shaky hands. This isn't happening. It can't be. But the burning in my shoulder is gone and it's pure relief.

I swallow hard and lower my hands, turning to glance at

the wound. Only when I do, it's different. It's . . . golden.

"Oh my God," I murmur, brushing at the skin, but nothing else comes off. It's a layer of gold, under the surface, gleaming in the yellow light of the streetlamps.

"No." I shake my head, not sure what's wrong with me. As if the Need isn't enough. Now my skin? What the hell is wrong with my skin? I blink rapidly and back away from the warehouse, rubbing roughly at my shoulder, trying to get rid of the spot. The gold.

I stumble off the curb and I'm immediately flooded in light from an oncoming car. I scream, holding my arms up in front of me, my white shirt still hanging off my shoulder. Tires squeal. Metal bangs against my thighs and I'm knocked back; the force of it driving me into the ground where my head smacks the pavement with a sick thud. Everything goes black.

"Yo, girl," I hear. "You alive?"

I blink slowly. No scene comes into focus. All I see is a glowing figure in front of me, a person outlined in light. He's staring down, alternating between yelling at me and yelling into his phone.

Despite the throbbing of my legs and the daggers in the back of my head, I sit up. My body burns, my bones pull toward the guy, toward his light. Although none of my other Needs have ever glowed like this, I know it's him. And suddenly images flash and I can see why I'm here.

"Francisco," I whisper, feeling some relief as I say his name. He jumps away from me, shaking his head.

"Do I know you?" he asks.

There is warm liquid trickling down my cheek and I touch it. It might be blood, but when I look at my hand I can't tell. All I can see is Francisco. And the impending shoot-out.

I can't distinguish his features but I can tell he's scared as he backs away. I groan, getting to my feet, ignoring the aching. I want to help him. I have to.

"You need to turn yourself in," I say, brushing absently at my blood-soaked hair. "The police know where you are. They're on their way." And I can see what will happen if he tries to run. I know they'll kill him.

"Who are you?" Francisco screams at me, taking his phone from his ear. I feel a jolt of fear as he thinks of striking me, but he doesn't. He's too frightened. "Who are you?" he asks again, his voice cracking.

"I'm no one," I murmur, the words startling me. My tone is so calm, and I don't feel like myself. All I feel is the Need.

In my head I can see Francisco dressed in black at the curb of a big stone house on the other side of town. He's younger than I'd thought, maybe twenty? While he waits, his fingers tap on the steering wheel as his best friend, Leo, is inside the home, robbing it.

Leo hadn't known the man was home. And he didn't mean to shoot him. Or at least, that's what Francisco tells himself. That's what he wants to think.

When he heard the shots, Francisco should have left, but he couldn't run. It's not the way. And he needed the money for his grandma. Leo had promised him 50 percent just to drive.

Here in the street Francisco grasps the handle of his car door. "I didn't do it," he calls out to me, as if he can't help but confess. "I wasn't in the house!"

I nod and move toward him, needing to touch him. His light is so bright as it glows with his emotions, but I can feel that he's not listening. He's not doing what he's supposed to. He's almost over.

"Please," I murmur, seeing his aura flicker toward me, as if reaching out to me. "It's time. Your grandma needs you alive. She won't survive if you go."

He cries out at the mention of his grandmother and runs his hands roughly through his short hair. Suddenly I can tell he's listening.

"Damn, girl," he murmurs, like he doesn't know what to do. He looks around the road, indecisively, and that's when I reach out. Not because I'm trying to, but because I have to. The vines are back, pulling me to him.

My hot hand touches his forearm and I feel the skin sear underneath, a surge running through both of us. He yanks back, but it's too late. He's been touched. He's felt it. He believes me.

Francisco is gasping as his aura fades from my vision. Now I can see that his hair is cropped short and there's a ring piercing his dark eyebrow. He's staring at me, his eyes glassy and trancelike, tears running down his cheeks. I see the fading mark of a handprint on his arm.

"What are you?" he asks, out of breath. "What the hell are you?"

His words hurt me, not like the hurt in my head, which is killing me right now. Not like the deep bruising I can feel in my legs as I stand here, half dazed. His words are exactly what I ask myself every night before I fall asleep. What am I?

I swallow hard. "I don't know," I whisper. "I'm no one."

I wait in the shadows of the alley until the cops arrive. It's only a matter of minutes, but in that time, Francisco calls his grandmother to confess and then calls his girlfriend, who is waiting for him back at their apartment. And now he's ready.

Three squad cars blare through the streets and stop in a zigzag around Francisco's car. My shirt is buttoned up, hiding *it*, and I realize that I've forgotten my new jacket at Harlin's. Which is just as well. It would have gotten filthy.

I watch as Francisco raises his arms above his head. No one seems to notice me among the flashing lights. I hear the cops radioing back to the dispatchers, saying they've caught the perp. I'm relieved. The shoot-out was avoided.

Francisco is bent over the hood of his car as he's handcuffed and the officer is reading him his rights. Then a chubby, short officer with his gun casually at his side leans toward Francisco.

"Surprised the hell out of me, son. Thought you'd be running all night. What made you stop here?"

I tense, hoping Francisco doesn't tell them about me. I don't want to have to explain this—the unexplainable. What would

I tell the cops? I'm a freak that's compelled to help people against my will? That I've tried to stop but it hurts too much? I can't explain what I don't know. I start to back away when I see Francisco blink, looking confused. Finally, he just mumbles, "I don't remember."

With that, I exhale, completely relieved. I start walking and as I'm about to turn onto Powell Street, I see something out of the corner of my eye. When I look, she's there, just on the other side of the street. The woman from the bus stop.

Her blond hair is a stark contrast against her black leather trench coat and boots. Cops are moving around but no one speaks to her. She's just watching me. I'm drawn to her, but I don't move. I'm feeling a little nauseated. When I think this, she smiles. Then she reaches behind her shoulder and pulls her hood up over her head, shading her eyes. She turns on her heels and walks away, the clacking of them on the pavement echoing through the street.

And then it begins to rain.

CHAPTER 5

amn it," I murmur, trying to duck in the doorway of an old building. I'm suddenly freezing without the Need, and my wet white blouse isn't helping the situation.

I wrap my arms around myself and wait a few minutes. Soon, just as suddenly as it started, the rain stops. I step away from the building, staring up at the night sky. The weather here isn't usually this unpredictable.

With a heavy sigh, I limp through the dark city streets, wishing a cab would come by, but remembering that I don't have the money to pay for a ride anyway. Each step is agony and I'm starving. But what's worse is that Francisco's words are still in my ears.

What are you?

I reach for my shoulder but then draw my hand away. I don't want to touch the golden spot. I'm terrified of what's happening to me.

I wish I really was just psychic. I wish I was anything. Because right now I feel so wrong—running out into the night instead of hooking up with my boyfriend. Knowing things I can't possibly know. Seeing people's souls! Despair hits me and I begin to cry, sniffling hard and rubbing at my cheeks. Maybe I'm cursed.

The sound of a motor cuts through the night from behind me and my muscles tense. Anyone out after dark is looking for trouble. At least, that's what Mercy would say. Careful not to be obvious, I glance over my shoulder toward the single oncoming light of a motorcycle.

Harlin. I nearly explode with relief. I recognize his bike and worn, brown leather jacket and wave at him. I feel saved.

He drives his bike hard into the curb, jumping off of it before it clangs to the ground. "What the hell, Charlotte?" he yells, running to me. "I've been looking for you all night!"

I move toward him, wanting him to hold me and tell me that I'm okay. But he stops short on the sidewalk, the color draining from his face. His eyes are wide with concern, but then he rushes forward and throws his arms around me. "What happened? Are you okay?"

I'm confused, but then I remember the accident. Smacking my head. The warm liquid that soaked my hair and traveled down my cheek. I probably look *really* bad.

"I got hit by a car," I answer quietly, watching him as he

examines me. I breathe deeply, comforted by his smell. I want to tell him about the Need, about the golden skin. But I don't. Because once I tell him I can't take it back and he'll know for sure that I'm a freak. How can he love someone whose skin is falling off?

"A car! Are you serious?" Harlin pulls back and looks me over from head to toe, just in case I'm missing a leg and he hasn't noticed before now. "Is anything broken? Didn't they stop?" He's shaking his head, overwhelmed. I close my eyes and lean into him, letting him wrap me up in his arms.

I'm too tired to make up a lie right now. "Can you take me to the clinic?" I ask, not lifting my head from his shoulder. The clinic will be closed soon. I really don't think anything is broken, but I'm bleeding from the head and the emergency room just seems like such a hassle. And then there's the issue of my skin. What if they see it? They might send me to Area 51 or some top-secret lab.

"Of course I'll take you." Harlin keeps his arm around me as he leads me to his motorcycle. "You should tell me why the hell you climbed out my fire escape," he mumbles. "But first, I think you need stitches."

I nod, not sure how I'll explain away tonight's disappearing act, but instead of worrying, I press my cheek against his chest as we walk to his bike.

"How do you get hit by a car on Broadway at this time of night?" Monroe asks in his British accent. He's treated all

kinds of injuries, but he definitely seems to get more serious when it's me—maybe because he's known me for so long.
With the situations the Need puts me in, it's not that rare for
me to require the occasional stitch or splint. I can usually avoid
the head trauma, though.

He continues with a long sigh. "I give you the night off and
you become a streetwalker? It's embarrassing, really."

I tell him to shut the hell up, but I'm glad he hasn't called
Mercy. She's going to have a coronary when she hears about
this. I still haven't thought of a way to explain why I was out.

I shift on the exam table, thinking of Harlin in the waiting
room. I'll have to tell him something. I just don't know what.

"Stay still, Charlotte," Monroe warns as he ties off the thread
and then grabs the scissors to snip it.

"Sorry." I sit on the crinkling paper while he cleans off the
metal tray and goes to the sink to wash his hands. When he first
examined me, Monroe was quick to give me a Vicodin after getting a look at the huge, bumper-sized bruises on my thighs. It's
left me a little groggy, but that's good. He told me I'd be really
sore for a few days, but that there was no permanent damage.

When I told him not to call the cops to report the accident,
he definitely eyed me suspiciously, scratching at his slightly
graying five o'clock shadow. But Monroe and I have known
each other forever—he trusts me. And I'm sure he'll expect
me to explain later.

When I was seven, I came into this clinic with a broken
arm that I'd gotten on the school playground. Max Rothsberg

didn't want to hear that I knew he'd stolen money out of the donation basket. Instead, he pushed me down and *snap!*

Oddly enough, a week later when I went back to school, he didn't remember even talking to me about it. He'd given the money back while I was gone. I tried to tell one of the nuns right when the Need happened, but she chalked it up to childhood delusions and scolded me for lying. She said that kids can't see visions—only God can. So after that I kept my mouth shut.

Mercy was volunteering at the clinic during those years and sometimes she'd bring me in with her. I liked hanging around. Monroe would talk with me about school. About my home life. It was nice sometimes, having a person other than Mercy care about me. Monroe's the closest thing to a father I've ever known. So when I turned twelve and Monroe asked me to volunteer, I was happy to say yes.

Just being here at the clinic, I feel a zillion times better. It's so familiar. Safe.

Monroe steps on the trash can, opening it with a metal clang. Just then, there's a small itch at my shoulder. At the spot. I know I have to tell someone about the mark on my skin. I can't keep this a secret. "Monroe," I whisper, my throat dry. He pauses while removing his gloves, and looks over. I'm sure he can hear in my voice that something is wrong.

"Are you hurt somewhere else?" He shifts in his loafers, darting his gaze over my body. With a quick snap he pulls off his gloves and tosses them on the counter.

"Um . . ." My cheeks start to warm because I'm not quite sure how to say it. I have no idea how to tell him that my skin is flaking away. "It's . . ." I can't look at him anymore, and my shoulders slump. I can't show him.

"Go ahead, Charlotte," he whispers. "It's okay."

I look up and he's watching me. It throws me off how he's waiting, his lips pressed together, his eyes narrowed intently. Could . . . could he know? I start to unbutton the silver tabs on my blouse. My heart is racing. I don't know what's going to happen next and I'm terrified.

I push the fabric away from my skin, from the spot, and I hear him gasp. My stomach drops and I regret showing him, but he's immediately next to me, running his finger over it, examining it. He's not wearing his gloves anymore and I wonder if he's grossed out.

"My God," he murmurs, putting his entire hand over the gold, covering it up. I'm ready to cry. What's wrong with me? But Monroe turns and his blue eyes are glassy. "It's so beautiful."

I blink quickly, feeling confused. "What?" I wonder if maybe I have a concussion, or if the Vicodin has made me loopy. There's no way he just called this beautiful. I'm missing skin. It's disgusting!

I push Monroe back and hurriedly button my blouse. Maybe I do need to go to the emergency room. But the minute I think it, there's a knot in my gut. They would want to perform tests, call in experts. The Need is one thing . . . but golden skin? That's not normal. Not even a little.

I raise my eyes to meet Monroe's and his face is stoic, frozen, amazed. He slowly starts to shake his head from side to side, a soft smile on his lips. "It's the most beautiful thing I've ever seen. It's finally happening. It's a miracle."

"*Happening?* What is happening to me? You have to—"

Just then the door opens and Monroe and I both turn toward it. Harlin looks between us as he eases his way in. "Hey," he says. "I wanted to check and see if everything was okay. You guys have been in here a while and I—" He stops, staring at Monroe. "She is okay, right?" Harlin's unshaven jaw is tight I can see he's about to burst from worry.

"Yes," I say quickly, and hop down from the table, the deep bruising of my thighs making me wince. "Monroe stitched me up. How many did I need again?" I try to sound light. It's more pretending. Lying. But I don't want Harlin to know about how the spot has changed. Not yet.

Monroe takes too long to answer and then finally, like coming out of a dream, he whispers, "Four stitches."

"Damn," Harlin says, putting his arms tenderly around me. "What were you doing out there? I'm gonna buy you an ankle monitoring bracelet."

I laugh.

"You're free to go," Monroe announces in a choked voice. He stares as if asking me to stay, but I can't. I'm overwhelmed and confused. I just want to leave with Harlin.

I don't talk as Monroe robotically recites stitch care instructions, and instead I just rest against Harlin. My mind is turning over Monroe's words, trying to understand why he called the spot beautiful. Why he didn't seem surprised or freaked out when he saw it.

When Monroe's done talking I turn in Harlin's arms, my body completely exhausted. "I'm starving," I say. "Can we go grab something to eat?"

He sighs, like it's the last thing he feels like doing. "It's after ten." When I bat my eyelashes, he laughs. "Fine, we'll go to Sid's. I think they're still open."

"Thanks, *honey*," I say.

"Don't pull out the 'honey.' That doesn't work on me."

"The eyelashes did."

He squeezes me and nuzzles his face into my neck. "I'm glad you're okay," he whispers against me, and I feel the playfulness slip away. My worry grows. Could Harlin love me if he knew what was wrong with me?

There's a sound of riffling papers and I look up to see Monroe holding sheets out to us. "Instructions," he says. "Call me if there are any new . . . developments."

I nod before taking Harlin's hand and turning toward the door. Just before we leave, I glance back at Monroe and he's watching me, his skin pale like he's just seen a ghost.

CHAPTER 6

I can't eat. Harlin's talking about how he'd driven all over the city looking for me, and I'm holding a greasy slice of cheese pizza, but I'm not listening. I'm staring out the window at the blinking Gold's Gym sign, only the 's is out, so it says: Gold. Gold. Gold.

I turn my head from side to side, trying to loosen the muscles in my neck. The Vicodin has made sounds echo in my ears and I'm starting to feel sleepy. I glance across the booth at Harlin and he's still talking, using his hands to accentuate how frantic he was during the search. And I smile because right now I have no Need. Just him.

"Hey," I whisper. He pauses, his eyes bloodshot, his mouth open. I just stare at him until he laughs and leans back in his seat, shaking his head.

"You're a handful, you know that, right? You make me completely crazy."

"I know," I say, and take a bite of pizza. "I make myself crazy."

"I'm not gonna just let this slide, Charlotte. Not this time. You have to tell me where you were going tonight."

I reach up to touch at my stitches, no idea how to answer. Sometimes I think it'd be worth losing him, just so I didn't have to worry about losing him. But I know I can't live without Harlin. I meet his eyes.

"I was checking out an old warehouse on Broadway," I say. "I saw the flyer in Plato's and I heard they were remodeling the building."

"What does that have to do with you?"

"Nothing. I . . . I thought maybe it'd be something you'd want to be involved with. Some original artwork for the lobby or something?"

Harlin looks me over like he's trying to decide if I'm telling the truth. "You don't mention anything to me? You just sneak out?"

"That was stupid. I'm sorry."

"Sorry," he repeats calmly. "I spent the night looking for you, completely freaking out. But you're sorry. That's nice, Charlotte." He goes back to eating his pizza, no longer looking at me.

I'm so tired that I feel like I could just confess everything to him. The nights I've been out. The things I've seen. The people I've saved.

Harlin's face is hard, but then he looks me over and his eyes weaken. It's like he just remembered I'm injured.

"Damn," he says. "I'm an ass."

"No, you're not."

"I am. I'm sorry."

I know that I'm the one who should be apologizing, but I take a bite of pizza instead. I just want to forget about today.

"How's your head?" Harlin asks, the softness of his voice making me melt a little.

"Hurty."

"And your legs?"

I smile. "Bruisy."

Harlin's foot touches mine, and heat shoots up my leg. I'd forgotten what we were doing just before I'd left his apartment. I bite my bottom lip and narrow my eyes. I want him. He reacts, taking in a breath, and then blows it out with frustration.

"Completely crazy," he says with a laugh. "And we're not . . ." He motions to my body, then groans longingly. "Not when you have stitches in your head."

"I'll have them for, like, two weeks."

He freezes, looks around the pizza place and then back to me. "Two weeks?"

"Uh-huh."

"All right, Charlotte," he orders, nodding toward my food. "Hurry up with that pizza. I'm not going home until I finish kissing you."

⤙ ✳ ⤚

"You sure?" Harlin asks, his mouth against mine as we stand in front of my building. "I could come in for a few minutes."

I kiss him back, my hands tangled under his coat in his T-shirt. His fingers find the bare skin just above my jeans and dig in, pulling me close. I sigh. "Can't tonight."

"No fun," he murmurs, not letting me go. "What if we fall asleep and Mercy comes home or something? She'd kill you. Like stab-your-balls dead."

He pulls his head back. "Mood killer, Charlotte."

I smile and peck his lips again before dropping my arms and motioning toward my apartment. "I should go in," I say. The night around us is dark and starless and Harlin is the only beautiful thing in sight.

"Tomorrow's going to suck for you," he says, glancing at my thighs as he backs toward the curb. "Call me when you get up. Maybe if you're a good girl I'll take you to VooDoo Donuts for a bacon maple bar."

I laugh. "You know me so well."

He winks and climbs on his bike. I stand, watching him leave, and I miss him the minute he's gone. I have reasons other than Mercy to not let Harlin upstairs, the main one being my golden skin. I have to find a way to fix it. I have to—

"Charlotte?"

I jump at the sound of the voice and turn quickly. Monroe walks up from the sidewalk, his car parked down a few buildings. He's still in his loafers and work clothes, so I wonder how long he's been waiting here. The clinic closed nearly two hours ago.

"You scared the crap out of me," I gasp. "Maybe you could have called first?"

"You didn't answer your phone."

I go to check my pocket and remember that I'd left my coat, with the phone in its pocket, at Harlin's.

"Can we talk inside?" Monroe asks, stepping closer. His blue eyes are serious and I'm suddenly frightened about what he's here to say.

But Monroe didn't run off when he saw my skin at the clinic. He's a doctor. And unless I want to become Oregon's newest science experiment, it seems that Monroe might be the only person who can help me.

I look him over, fear and anticipation prickling my skin, and then I take out my key and lead us inside.

Sitting uncomfortably on the wooden stool at the kitchen counter, I face the living room as Monroe searches through his coat pockets, looking for something. No one else is home. Mercy's working, Alex is with his boyfriend, Reggie, at a party somewhere in the Pearl, and Georgia . . . she's wherever it is that she goes at night. Right now there's just me, Monroe, and the hum of the refrigerator.

"Ah," he says as he pulls a small black journal out of his pocket and takes a pen from inside the worn pages. I've seen him write in it before. His medical journal. He jots something down and then sets it next to him on the couch. After a long pause, he looks over at me.

"I've been waiting for you," he says softly. "I'm glad you've finally come."

My black shoe slips off the rung of the stool and I almost fall. When I right myself, I'm shaking. "What are you talking about? You're freaking me out!" My fingers tremble as I grasp the edge of the counter, trying to keep steady.

"Don't be scared." He holds up his palms, his expression full of compassion. But I *am* scared. I'm terrified. "I'm going to help you through this."

"Through what?" I demand. "What's wrong with me?"

"Wrong with you?" He laughs to himself, though his eyes are shining with tears. "That's the thing, sweetheart. This isn't wrong—even if it feels that way right now."

I'm offended that he'd even say that. I push my shirt off my shoulder, exposing the golden area. "Look at me!" I yell, but a new worry grips me. Doctors don't make house calls like this. "Wait. Are you here because I'm dying? Oh God. Am I dying?" I cover my mouth with my hand. I start to cry until I notice the tears brim over his eyes and run down his cheeks. He looks away from me, wiping harshly at them.

"Please don't," he says, his voice cracking. "Don't cry, Charlotte. You must be strong right now. This is going to be very difficult and you have to be strong."

Dozens of diseases run through my mind. Cancer, MS, leprosy. "Please," I whisper. "Help me."

"I'm trying."

We sit quietly for a second, both sniffling. Then Monroe clears his throat and picks up his medical journal, placing it back in his jacket pocket. He pulls out a bottle of pills and shakes two into his hand. He tosses them into his mouth and swallows them dry. After he puts the bottle away, he turns to me, his face solid and serious. "There's nothing wrong with you," he says. "At least, not in the way that you think."

I'm partly relieved, but I know it can't be true. "I don't understand," I say. "It's not just the gold under my skin. I'm compelled to talk to people I've never met. Know things about them. It's creepy."

"You're helping them," he says.

"You know about that?" My heart rate explodes. Does Monroe know about everything? How can he know? "Are you like me?" I'm suddenly hopeful, but then Monroe shakes his head.

"No, sweetheart. I'm not. You . . . you're so much more."

I want to start crying again. My head is killing me and my legs are so sore I want to curl up and die. But I hold the tears back as Monroe watches me. "Stop being so cryptic and tell me what's wrong with me," I plead.

He presses his lips together. "I'll tell you what I can. But I'm confused about something—how, after all this time, you still don't know what you are. Has the answer never come to you?"

"I don't know what you're talking about," I murmur.

He leans forward on the couch, putting his elbows on his knees. "Usually by now you would have known. Felt the answer in your heart, maybe?" He looks away as if considering the thought. "Unless . . . you wouldn't believe?" Monroe seems content with talking to himself but I'm completely lost in the conversation. I can't figure out what he knows about the Need.

"Monroe, please. I don't understand. Do you know what this is or not?"

"I do," he says softly. "And I knew the minute I treated you nearly ten years ago. I saw that you were different when I X-rayed your arm."

"Wait," I say. "Is it cancer?" Mercy's mother died of breast cancer a few years ago and it was awful. Traumatizing. I nearly crumble at the idea of Mercy having to go through something similar with me. In fact, when I was a kid, Monroe used to test my blood for all sorts of things. He said my bones were weak. Is this why?

"No, no," Monroe says. "You're not sick."

"Then what did you see in my bones?"

He smiles to himself. "I wasn't sure I'd recognize it again— I thought I'd lost the sight. But when your X-ray came back, it showed the break—the light seeping from it. And I knew you." He pauses. "Not *you* exactly. But your kind."

A hot streak of terror races through me. "My *kind*? What the hell does that mean?"

"It's okay," Monroe soothes. "You're not dying, Charlotte. You're just . . . changing."

I grab on to the counter again, holding myself up. "Changing into what?"

"The Forgotten."

I stare at him, anger and fear welling up inside me. "What is that?"

"You have a destiny, Charlotte. A purpose. The Forgotten save people, they save souls. You're like a gift to Earth."

I can feel the color draining from my face. "There's no such thing."

Monroe winces. "Forgive me," he murmurs. "I'm usually much better prepared." He rubs roughly at his hair, darting his gaze around the room. "I thought it'd be easier than this," he says, as if I know what he's talking about. "I thought since we were close . . ."

"I don't understand."

He nods. "I know. But listen to me, this is a wonderful blessing."

"I don't feel very blessed."

"A blessing for *us*. Because you've come." He adjusts his position on the couch to better face me, but I'm barely staying on the stool. I feel like I might pass out. "The Forgotten," he says. "They lead us toward the light, toward the good. You're unconditional love, forgiveness. Guidance. You're here to help."

"But . . . it's killing me," I stammer. "I'm in pain. And now my skin—"

"I'll help you through the pain and loss. I've been helping your kind my entire life, Charlotte. I've traveled the world looking for them, studying them, helping them cross over. I'm a Seer. I'm here to lead you home," he whispers, bowing his head.

"No," I say, suddenly overcome with loss. I've always thought Monroe could solve anything. He takes care of my cuts and broken bones, he helps with my research papers when Mercy has to work late. But now he's just letting me go when I need him.

I jump down from the stool and dash over, dropping at Monroe's feet. "Please, help me." I clench my hands in front of me. "Please."

His face scrunches with sadness as he reaches out and puts his hands over mine. "It's your destiny," he says. "I'm sorry, but I can't stop it."

I suck in a breath and wipe at my tears. Monroe knew all along that I was different, but never told me. It makes me wonder what else he doesn't tell me. It makes me wonder about him.

I'm not sure what to believe anymore. Still on the floor, I slide back from him. I wrap my arms around my knees and stare, feeling devastated. "What does this mean? Is more of my skin going to fall off?" I ask.

"Yes."

I whimper, the horror of it nearly too much. "What else? What else is going to happen to me?"

Monroe pauses. "The Forgotten are sent from the light to live among us. And as you save people, continuing your destiny, this body will wear away. The energy will build inside you until you're gone completely—a brilliant burst of light that's more beautiful that anything you can ever imagine. You'll leave us all with your love."

I gasp. "It *is* going to kill me."

He shakes his head. "No. It's going to set you free. It'll let you go from this form so that you can spread your light, your love. You save lives."

"I don't want to save anybody," I say. "You're wrong. It's not true." And suddenly I just want him to leave. To leave me alone so that I can lie down, rest my body. Everything hurts, but it only reminds me of how much I want to keep my skin. Forget the light. I won't go.

I stand up, flinching as I put pressure on my thighs. "Good night," I say to Monroe, and walk toward the apartment door. I open it but don't turn around. I don't want to see that adoring look he has for the gold on my shoulder. When I don't hear him move I say good night again, only louder. He gets up.

Monroe Swift—doctor extraordinaire—pauses in front of me, his blond eyebrows pulled together in concern. I used to think he could save the world. I used to think he cared for me.

"Soon you'll understand," he says.

I glare at him, angry. Scared. He nods and starts out the door. "Monroe?" I call. He stops and glances over his shoulder. "Why are they called the Forgotten?"

His eyes weaken, like he might cry. But instead, he clears his throat. "You'll know soon enough, sweetheart." He looks at the ground and then to me. "Let's keep this between us, shall we?" he asks.

"Like anyone would believe me." I touch the stitches, mostly to check that they're still there. That this is still happening.

I close my eyes, listening to the sound of his shoes slapping on the tiles. And when it's quiet, I close the door and lean against it.

Even though I'm mad that Monroe has been keeping secrets from me, I want to believe that he won't let anything happen to me. No matter what he says now, he won't just let me die. I've known him since I was a kid. He's friends with Mercy. He's friends with *me*.

And he's the only person who can help me.

Feeling unsteady, I stumble across the room to the couch. Even if Monroe is wrong about my skin, it doesn't explain the Need. It doesn't explain why I'm consumed with helping people I don't know.

I yawn, feeling exhausted and overwhelmed. I'll get more answers, but not tonight. I glance at the clock on the wall and see that it's after midnight. I close my eyes, hoping that in the morning things will go back to normal . . . or as normal as they were yesterday. Which, admittedly, isn't all that normal.

CHAPTER 7

I'm startled awake by the sound of keys jingling in the apartment door. As it slowly opens I sit up, the dried tears on my cheeks leaving my skin feeling stiff. Georgia walks in, but pauses. She looks at me and then around the apartment.

"Mercy still at work?"

I nod.

"Cool." She shuts the door behind her and turns the deadbolt before shrugging off her gray coat. "What are you doing up?" she asks, tossing her jacket over a chair. She drops down across from me and bunches her short dark hair into a ponytail on top of her head with an elastic band she's been wearing around her wrist.

"I had a rough night," I say.

69

"Boyfriends suck." She sighs. "Especially the cute ones."

We've never talked about Harlin, really, but she did mention once that he was *sexy as hell*. It made Alex and me giggle at the time. Weird that I never asked if she had a boyfriend. "Are you seeing someone?"

She tsks. "I got a guy waiting on me back home. I don't have time for the fools around here." She pauses. "No offense."

"None taken."

"So what did your man do? He find another girl?"

I shake my head. "I was actually hit by a car tonight."

Her dark eyes widen. "You okay?"

"Few stitches, but I'm fine."

She seems to think this over, then nods and rests her head back into the chair and closes her eyes. "You're crazy, girl."

After six months I feel like this is the most heartfelt conversation Georgia and I have ever had. We don't fight; barely even talk, really. It's just that I'm always wrapped up in Harlin or the Need, and she's . . . doing what she does.

When Georgia first came here, Alex was totally jealous. He's been with Mercy since he was a baby, and he takes every opportunity to still act like one. So when Mercy gave Georgia driving lessons before him, Alex went berserk. And Georgia, being sort of a badass, told him off. Now they make a sport of it.

All I know is that Georgia's mom will be out of prison soon, and when she is, Georgia will move back with her. Maybe that's why I haven't tried to get to know her.

I feel suddenly guilty, especially after what Monroe told me. I'm supposed to be some sort of angel, and yet I've ignored my foster sister for months.

I stare at Georgia, wondering what it's like to have a mother you could remember, and then lose her. Wondering if she thinks about her mom all day as she waits for her. Georgia's dark skin is dotted with old acne marks and her multi-ringed fingers start to brush back her hair. When she turns her head, I see it. Her scar.

It's pink and jagged and it runs from behind her ear all the way down to her jaw. I'd noticed it the first day she showed up here, but no one's ever asked her about it. I think we all just assumed it had to do with why she was in foster care to begin with. I'm struck by the fact that I don't know. That I live with her and know nothing about her.

"What happened to your neck?" I ask.

She looks up and stares back at me viciously. "None of your damn business, Charlotte. Did I ask why you were out late getting hit by cars when you're supposed to be at home?"

I'm stunned, feeling embarrassed. "No. You didn't. I'm sorry."

We're quiet for a minute and I'm about to go to bed when Georgia starts talking, her eyes closed and her head turned away.

"When I was fifteen," she says, "my mother was into drugs—using and selling. And one time she let the wrong people in." She sucks at her teeth as if the memory is painful. "Mom got hit a couple of times, but I got the worst of it. Five stab wounds and a broken collarbone. Spent three weeks in the hospital." Georgia looks over at me. "After that my mom got arrested for possession and I've been bounced from house to house. But I'm almost eighteen and my mom's getting out in a few weeks and we're starting over. She's clean now."

I'm amazed that she told me this, but I'm without words. Georgia had been attacked. Brutalized. Why hadn't the Need sent me to her? Why didn't I save her instead of some junkie in an alley or a thug running from the cops? It doesn't seem fair. Nothing seems fair anymore.

"I'm sorry," I say finally.

She waves me off. "Now never ask me again."

I press back into the couch, watching her as she rests, looking too tired to make it to her room. And I wish that I could somehow save her.

But mostly I wish that I could save myself.

There are sounds around me, but whenever I try to open my eyes, I sink underwater again, submerged in the thickness of sleep that won't let me go.

"I don't know," I hear Georgia say. "She was talking about getting hit by a car."

"Is she dead?" Alex asks as I feel an arm wrap around my shoulders and tug me forward.

"You're a damn fool. You can see her breathing right there."

Alex gasps, and there's a whisper of a touch on my head.

"Oh, yeah. Look, she has stitches."

"Let me see."

"Right there."

And then I'm out, surrounded in dark. But in the distance there is a small glow, a tiny light. Suddenly I'm standing alone, the space starting to brighten as the light grows.

"It's going to hurt, you know?"

I jump at the sound of the voice and look sideways. Standing next to me in the dark is the woman in black. Up close she's even more beautiful than I thought—icy blue eyes, pale porcelain skin. And her voice has the slightest hint of a Russian accent.

"That light"—she motions toward it—"hurts like hell. Worse than being burned alive."

"Who are you?" I ask.

"I'm like you." She grins widely. "Only more evolved." She stops suddenly and looks around, as if she heard something that I didn't. She meets my eyes. "We'll talk more soon."

My eyes flutter and I feel a jolt. I'm lying flat in my bed.

"Finally," Alex says. I turn to see him sitting on the edge of the mattress, pushing my legs. "Thought maybe you did die."

I swallow hard, startled by my dream . . . by the woman. The smell of bacon is in the air and I'm comforted by home. I'd know the lingering smell of Mercy's cooking anywhere. Within a few seconds the dream starts to fade.

"No," I say, my voice thick with sleep. "I'm alive. Got the bruises to prove it." I reach up to feel my head, the stitches still poking out. "My brain hurts," I murmur.

Alex chuckles and grabs a cup of water off my dresser and holds it out to me. "Your savior is here," he says after I take the glass, and he tosses me a bottle of Advil.

"Hallelujah." I down three pills, and then think better and take one more.

"Your man has been calling this house all morning," Alex says. "You'd better call him back before he sends the SWAT team." He picks at his nails. "And we don't need that kind of trouble. Georgia might have someone tied up and gagged in her room."

I burst out laughing and then wince, touching at my scalp. I kick him off the bed. "Georgia's not that bad," I say. "She and I had a sisterly heart-to-heart last night."

Alex shrugs. "Oh, so you like her better now?" He says it jokingly, but I can hear the tension in his voice. Once you've been a foster kid, I'm not sure you can ever be loved enough. And although Mercy gives Alex the world, I think he's still scared of being abandoned. I know I am.

"What time is it?" I ask.

"After ten."

"Damn." Classes started two hours ago, so it looks like I'm taking the day off. I hope St. Vincent's hasn't tried to call Mercy at work. I haven't even told her I'd been in an accident yet. I gnaw on my lip, trying to count out when she'll get home from her fourteen-hour shift.

Alex sighs. "I have to go. Today we're doing highlights." I

make a face at him because he's lucky. While I have to attend St. Vincent's at eight a.m. every morning, he gets to take classes at vocational school—highlights and weaves from twelve to three. Really I just think he goes because he likes to have half days.

The house phone rings from my dresser, and Alex rolls his eyes. "Romeo again. Want me to grab it?"

"Will you?"

Alex snatches the phone and passes it over. I glance at the caller ID. "It's actually Sarah," I say.

"Ugh. Can't stand that girl." Alex flees because the sound of Sarah's perky voice is like nails on a chalkboard to him. He thinks she's a spoiled brat, she thinks he's a bitter foster kid. They're both sort of right, so I don't get involved.

"Thank you," I sing as he walks out the door.

I smile and click on the phone. "Hello, dear."

"What. The. Hell. I'm at school, Charlotte. Where are you?"

"In bed."

"Clearly. Now get up. I have major problems and I need you here." I instantly feel bad for not being there for her. Sarah has a way of guilting me into things. It's her gift.

I sit up, my head feeling like it's two seconds behind my movements. But I'm thinking forward to the quickest way to school, bus or cab. "Are you okay?" I ask.

"What? I'm fine. Sort of. So last night at the charity event, something happened. And I cannot deal with this today. Not by myself."

I relax a little. I realize that her voice isn't frantic enough for this to be an actual emergency. This is a Sarah emergency, which means it relates to boys, clothes, or boys. "You scared the crap out of me, you know?"

She snorts. "Hello? You didn't show up for school and Harlin's been calling me like a crazed maniac talking about how you were hit by a car. How are you feeling, by the way?"

"Nice of you to ask. I'm fine."

"Oh, please. If you were dead I would have found out long before now. Besides, I called Monroe the second I heard and he said you were fine. So don't get all feel-sorry-for-me. Now are you going to help me or not?"

"Sarah, I'm ninety-nine percent sure that I can't help you. But if you need me to listen while you complain, I can do that."

"Awesome. Meet me for lunch at Frankie's. My treat."

"I just woke up. I have stitches in my head!" But somehow I know that even this isn't a good enough excuse to miss lunch.

"See you in twenty," she hangs up.

I put the phone down on my bed and rub roughly at my face. Sarah knows it will take me longer than twenty minutes to get to Frankie's, and that's if I don't shower. But I sigh and climb out of bed, wincing once when I put weight on my thighs.

I pause, last night's conversation with Monroe rushing back to me. The Forgotten. I stumble backward onto my bed, my heart racing. Quickly I shove my shirt off my shoulder and stare at the glowing gold beneath. My mind races through

76

everything he said. He said it wouldn't kill me. He said—

I'm like you. Only more evolved.

The voice in my head is from my dream, even though the memory of it is foggy along the edges. I can't quite remember, like it's just out of reach. I can still hear those words, though. I can still hear that voice.

I furrow my brow, considering what it means. Monroe had said that "they" should have told me by now. Maybe that's what the voice is. Maybe it'll tell me who I am and how I can save myself. If there's someone else like me out there, it means I don't have to die, right? Maybe I'm not the light after all. I feel almost relieved, so I stand and begin walking to the bathroom to get ready to meet Sarah. For the first time since finding the gold, I have a sense of hope. I'll get the answers and then I can—

The force of it hits me. A shiver that runs from my toes to the top of my aching head. An intense burning in my shoulder. A vine that twists around my gut.

The Need. It's back.

CHAPTER 3

I stumble out of my room, something pulling me fiercely toward the door. I'm still in my pajamas, barefoot. As I pass the kitchen, I hear Alex.

"Where are you going? I think you should wait for Mercy."

I'm burning up from the inside, needing to get out. I look sideways at him and try to smile. "Can't. Tell her I'll call her later."

"Not your secretary." He shakes his head and turns to open the fridge. I'm glad that he doesn't notice my bare feet. If he did, he might try to stop me. But there's somewhere I have to be. My body is demanding it.

As I get to the front door, a burst of wind blows through me and I pause. I still feel pulsing under my skin, in my shoulder.

But this is where I'm supposed to stop. I open my apartment door and peer out into the hallway. It's empty.

I stand there, not sure what to do. Is it Alex? Maybe I could just go back and grab my shoes, still make it to Frankie's. I'm about to try when I hear the squeak of hinges. I glance down the hallway and see the door of apartment 5468 ajar, but no one comes out. I'm not sure I've ever seen who lives there.

The Need pulls me out and I shut my door quietly, the sound of my bare feet padding on the floors. The door to the other apartment is still open.

I wheeze, heat searing my shoulder, and I push my T-shirt aside to look at the spot. It's glowing.

"Oh God," I murmur, trying not to cry. Unlike a few moments ago, the skin around the spot is now peeling at the edges; my skin rubbed away, exposing more gold. It's the size of a grapefruit, my entire shoulder an inhuman shade with an indescribable shine.

I tremble with the horror of my transformation. I'm wearing away, just like Monroe said I would. What if it can't be stopped and the gold reaches my face? How can I live? I lean against the faded green wall, feeling like I've just been punched in the gut. I don't want to go anywhere. I want to ball up and cry until I'm cured. But the Need rips me forward and I stumble down the hall again.

When I hear the creaking of a door, I stop. My breath comes out in short jagged gasps and my skin feels as if it's burning off.

There is a little girl in the doorway—her long blond hair

loose and wild around her face. She looks frightened.

"Hi," I say, unsure. Suddenly there is a burst of wind and I stagger forward, hoping I can help her. Hoping she can make this stop.

She doesn't answer and instead stares at me with wide blue eyes. My body aches, but I squat down in front of her, getting to her level.

"What's your name?" I ask. I wait but I can't see her past. Her want. She's just a little girl in front of me. But I can tell by the pulsing that this is where I'm supposed to be. Only, it's not her.

"I'm Olivia," she says in a tiny voice.

"Hi, Olivia." I smile, waiting for something to happen. The little girl reaches to wipe her nose with the back of her hand. "Are you alone?" I ask tentatively after a moment of awkward silence. She shakes her head.

I'm considering my next move, when I hear it. It's a soft moan from inside. The hairs on the back of my neck stand up and I try to look past her into the apartment. But it's dark, the windows blocked with heavy blankets.

I lean closer to Olivia. "Who's in there?"

Her mouth twitches. "My mom." There's another moan from behind her, this one followed by a gurgling sound. My vision starts to blur and I know I have to get inside.

"Take me to her," I say, reaching out to hold the little girl's hand. I'm unsteady and I wonder if my head smack last night has changed the way the Need works. It's unusual for me to be so weak.

"But Mommy doesn't want to—"

"Now," I say roughly, pushing open the door. The entire room is on a tilt, slowly tipping from one side to the next. The images are fuzzy. The little girl a blur in front of me. An eerie calm comes over me, but just below the surface, I'm scared. Scared that Monroe was right and I might slip away and dissolve right here.

Olivia doesn't say anything as she leads me into her apartment. The cracked plaster walls are bare. The smell is rancid, like rotting food. I glance toward the kitchen and see a sink of overflowing dishes before my vision starts to fade into darkness. I gasp. This has never happened before, not like this. I'm blind.

From somewhere in the apartment, I can hear moaning. The little girl is holding my hand, and I squeeze it, completely dependent on her for direction.

"She's on the floor over there," Olivia whispers and lets go of me. Just then, a weak yellow light surrounding a figure comes into focus. It's her. My Need.

I stumble toward her, wondering if now all of my Needs will involve glowing light. I hope that my vision will come back after I do what I'm here for. But what if it doesn't? I swallow hard and push the thought away. My body pulls me toward the edge of the room.

"Are . . . are you okay?" I ask the person lying on the apartment floor, when suddenly my mind is filled with images. Her name is Callie. I first see her as a young girl, her golden blond hair in pigtails. But the man touching her is much older, and it's as if I am her. I'm being molested.

I cringe, whimpering at the images when the next one flashes by and I'm in high school, injecting heroin into my arm and sighing as I lean back into a dirty couch. There are users and dealers all around me, groping me. But I don't care. Just as long as I'm not home.

It's a few years later and my belly is round, but I'm happy. I've never been so happy. And then the images change. I can see Callie again, her hair brushed and clean, as she walks hand in hand with a little girl—Olivia. They're smiling and laughing. I tilt my head, wondering what could have happened since then to make Callie an addict again.

Then I see *him*, the man who touched Callie when she was younger. He's older now, bushy mustache, pale blue sweater. He's standing with a woman who looks like Callie . . . her mother. I suck in a gasp of air. Her stepfather abused her. But her mother doesn't know. She never told her.

Olivia, close to the age she is now, comes running through the picture to get picked up by the man. He and her grandmother laugh and dote on her. She looks happy. But . . . where's Callie? Why would she let her daughter go with the man who—

My vision changes and I see Callie on her couch in this apartment just last week, wearing only a dirty tank top and underwear. She's reading a paper, a court order. She's lost custody. To them.

The images speed up, a montage of a week of drug-binging on heroin. Callie is afraid to tell her mother about her step-father, afraid it was her fault, afraid no one will believe her. And now . . . now her daughter might suffer the same thing. But she's denied it for so long, she's not even sure if it really happened anymore.

But it did. It definitely did. I stifle a cry because I still feel like it happened to me. I feel violated.

I shudder and then the images stop. Instead my vision returns and Callie's in front of me on the floor, her light flickering. She's overdosed on her latest batch of heroin. I want to save her—take away the pain. I kneel down, and reach out to brush back her filthy hair; it's dry and stiff. When I touch the crook of her arm where the needle went in, she gasps and opens her eyes. They go out of focus, staring past me.

I lean close and whisper. "Callie." My voice is calm. Comforting. "It wasn't your fault. What he did wasn't your fault. But you need to get well. You need to protect your daughter."

"Olivia," she murmurs.

"Yes." I squeeze her arm and the drugs run from her vein. Something is causing it, something beyond me. "You need help," I say. "And you need to tell the police. You need to tell your mother."

She starts to cry, shaking her head. "I can't. She'll hate me."

I know what I have to say, and it hurts. The thought fills me, compelling me to talk. "She already does." And it's unbelievable the lies that her mother has told herself over the years. How she's always resented Callie for demanding attention, for being on drugs. How even if she was told, her mother would still hate her, call her a liar. Stand by her husband.

My eyes well up as I imagine Callie's pain, her heart aching for freedom. Olivia is the only thing in her life she's ever cared about. Olivia is her only piece of love, and she might lose her forever.

"Callie," I say again, feeling my skin heat up, feeling it burn into hers. "You have to do this. You have to save Olivia."

Her body jerks away, whether from the burning or from my words, I'm not sure. But in a swaying, barely conscious movement, she holds the wall and tries to sit. She's sobering up. "Baby?" she calls out.

Out of the corner of my eye I see Olivia streak across the room to her mother, falling into her arms. But the Need doesn't go away. I feel that even if Callie fights, she'll lose. She'll lose her daughter no matter what.

But the Need's message is changing, coiling up and vibrating through me. When I know what the Need wants me to say, I try to refuse. It's not right. There has to be justice. I feel like I was the one abused and I want that bastard to pay, to spend his life in prison. But I have to tell Callie to do something different, something illegal. I grit my teeth, holding the message in, but it's like my stomach is twisting around itself, squeezing me until I groan.

"Run." The more I try to resist talking, the more constricted

I feel. I double over in pain. "You need to run," I say finally.

There's immediate relief, but I'm still weak. I can't believe what I've told her to do. I can't believe that it's right.

Callie manages to stand up, Olivia in her arms. She leans against the wall briefly before rushing over to the bedrooms. She's packing. The Need fades until it's gone.

What have I done?

I try to move, but I'm too weak, too sore. I have to crawl toward the door. I just want my bed. I'm nearly there, when I hear the pattering of feet. I look over my shoulder at Olivia. She's wearing sneakers and a coat; no longer in her pajamas. Her hair's been brushed and pulled into a ponytail. I try to summon a vision of their future, but can't see where they're running to. My connection to them is gone.

"Thank you," she says with a little smile. "My mom's taking me on a vacation."

I nod, conflicted. Everything in society tells me this is wrong, but I think I'm beginning to see something. That legal justice isn't always possible. It's a dismal thought and I swallow it down, trying to stand.

Olivia helps me, holding my elbow. I smile at her, run my hand over her hair. She'll be safe. In the end, isn't that all that matters? Aren't she and Callie saved?

I limp out the front door, using the green wall to support me as I walk down the hallway. Olivia waves to me as I slowly back away. I smile, knowing how completely the Need has changed the course of her life, and how I was a part of it. But what does that make me? An angel? Or something else entirely . . . ?

The apartment door opens wider and Callie is there, holding a small suitcase, a backpack over her shoulder. "Let's go," she says. She looks clean. Sober.

She glances at me. Her eyebrows knit together in concern. "You okay?" she asks cautiously, as if she's seeing me for the first time. I nod, and she puts her hand protectively on Olivia's shoulder.

She watches me another second, like maybe I remind her of someone, and then she closes her door but doesn't bother locking it. She won't be coming back.

"Come on," she whispers to Olivia and takes her daughter's hand. As they rush past me the little girl calls out, "Bye!" Her mother pulls her closer.

"Don't talk to strangers," she whispers harshly. The little girl seems confused but obeys and turns around.

It's then that it occurs to me and I can't believe I've never thought of it before. Whenever I help people, they don't seem to remember me. I used to think they were in shock, or they didn't want to admit what they'd been through. But thinking about the Needs, dating all the way back to Max Rothsburg, they didn't remember me. They forgot me.

My stomach drops. I am a Forgotten.

CHAPTER 9

I go back into my apartment, ignoring Alex's questions, and crash in my bed. I'm starving but too drained to do anything about it. Sarah will have to wait. I can't leave; I'm too weak. I drift off, dreaming of Callie, Francisco . . . all the faces I've seen over the years. And then I see a bridge with a woman sitting casually on a railing. It's the woman in black, and around us the world is quiet. Dead.

"Hello, Charlotte," she says, picking at the fingers of her leather gloves. "Any of this look familiar to you?"

Standing on the pavement, I feel nauseated. The next moment she discreetly waves her hand and the pain is gone. I'm fine. She looks back at me like she's waiting for an answer.

"This . . . this is the Rose City Bridge," I murmur. My voice

sounds raspy, like I'm asleep. It occurs to me that maybe I
still am.

"Very good." She watches me for a long moment and I want
to ask her so many questions, but I can't seem to form the
words. Everything feels so slow. I can barely move.

"Who are you?" I finally ask. She seems impressed.

"Onika." She holds out her glove but I'm moving slowly
and she pulls away before I can shake it. "You know," she
begins with a smile. "I've been looking for you for a long time,
Charlotte. Been following Monroe for . . ." She pauses to think.
"At least nine years. Where've you been, love?"

"Here. I've always been in Portland." I feel the first drop of
water hit my cheek and I look up to see storm clouds gathering
above us.

Onika tilts her head, her blond hair cascading over her
shoulder. She's beautiful. "I couldn't find you," she sings. "It's
been quite a Forgotten dry spell around here. They must have
been hiding you."

"Who was hiding me?"

"The powers that be, I guess. But they can't help you." She
hops down from the railing and the nausea returns, but this
time Onika does nothing to stop it. "I can."

"You can help me?"

There's a crackle of thunder that shakes the bridge. Above
us, the clouds part slightly to let down the sunlight. It lands on
me and I can't believe how warm it is. How inviting.

Onika smirks and turns away to walk across the bridge, her

88

boots echoing on the pavement. "Damned sunshine," she says without looking back. "Seems it's time for you to wake up." She snaps her fingers.

I jolt awake, feeling like I've just been dropped into my bed. I'm completely disoriented as I try to work through my dream. But it's fading fast. Was that real? Is Onika real? The handle of my bedroom door starts to turn and I'm frozen in place. Is she here?

Sarah's head pops in the door and she raises a perfectly shaped eyebrow at me.

"Wow," she says, before pushing the door all the way open. I feel like I haven't seen her in days, weeks. "You look like hell," she adds.

"Thanks." My heart rate slows and I try to sit up, the last bits of my dream nearly gone. I touch the stitches in my head. They're still there. And they still really hurt.

"I waited at Frankie's forever," Sarah starts. "Thanks and all. Then I decided that if you were too screwed up to meet me, you must be really bad off. So I had my driver bring me here. Mom took the Beamer today. Oh," she says, reaching her arm out, clutching a white paper bag, "I brought you a burger. But it's probably cold by—"

I jump forward and grab it from her hands, tearing into the bag. I'm ravenous. I take out the sandwich and push it into my mouth without saying anything. It's delicious. When I look up, Sarah's staring at me like I'm an animal at the zoo. "What?" I say with a full mouth.

"Uh, nothing, *tiger*. You're sure tearing into that meat."

I look down and see ketchup running down my hand, bits of bun and lettuce lying in my lap, on my comforter. "Oh." I demurely (if it's possible at this stage) reach into the bag and take out a napkin, dabbing at the corners of my mouth.

"Much better," she says sarcastically before pulling a chair from my desk and taking a seat next to me. "So are you really okay?" And for the first time, I see that she's worried. Complete, freaking-out worried.

I nod. "I'll be fine." But my words are hollow. I don't know if I'm okay, but I do know that I need to talk to Monroe again. He has to tell me what he's holding back. I have to believe that there's a way to keep me from disappearing into light. "What time is it?" I ask.

Sarah glances down at her delicate silver watch. "Almost three."

I nod and try to get up. "I have to go by the clinic and talk with Monroe. I think he's there now."

"You're well enough to see him, but not me?"

"He's my doctor."

She sighs. "And I'm your best friend. Totally uncool."

"I have some things I have to do—"

"And I need a friend right now!" Suddenly her eyes begin to well up and I know that I've missed something big. Something about last night.

I reach out to grab her sleeve, pulling her over to sit with me on the bed. "What happened?"

She rolls her eyes, as if she doesn't want to tell me now. "You should have foreseen it," she murmurs. But I've told her before, I'm not psychic. My problems are so much bigger than having a few visions. So much worse.

I wait only a second before Sarah starts talking. "I saw Seth last night."

"That's good. I thought that was the whole upside of going to the dinner."

She pauses, and meets my eyes. "It was. And he was happy to see me. Very happy." She looks away and I'm confused, but I decide not push it. To let her tell me in her own way.

"Okay."

"Things started off great," she says. "He told me I looked beautiful and asked if I'd go outside on the patio. And since the dinner was dull as hell, I said yes. The weather was so nice, we started walking the grounds. I followed him over to the side of the hotel." Her mouth pulls into a sad smile. "He asked if he could kiss me."

Normally, this would be a totally squealy moment, but by the way Sarah's talking, I know it's not. I know she's ashamed. And my stomach turns with anxiety.

"I'm not a good girl by any stretch of the imagination," she says. "So I said yes, pushed him up against the wall, and we started going at it." She looks at me. "He's a terrible kisser, by the way."

"I could've guessed that. He's a mouth breather." Maybe not really, but she's my friend and I've got her back.

"Anyways . . ." She sighs. "In another 'what the hell was I thinking' moment, he asked me to do more. I did. And after we returned to the dinner, I didn't feel too offended when we separated to opposite sides of the room. I figured he had his obligations. I had mine. But then"—she stops to hold up her finger—"as he's leaving, he comes over to me, leans in close, and whispers, 'That was great. Thanks.'"

The joking is gone. All that's left is humiliation and I feel it for her. It's not the same knowing that I get with the Need. This knowledge is from being someone's best friend. From knowing their every insecurity. I wish the Need would have stopped her from going to that dinner last night.

"So today," she says with a sad smile, "well, today is all about Sarah Sterns, the BJ queen. I should really have business cards made."

I drop my eyes, ready to cry. At St. Vincent's your reputation is all you have, both to the other students and the nuns. There's a chance that Sarah's mother (or God forbid, father) could get a call this afternoon, outlining the rumors.

"I'll have Harlin kick his ass," I say quickly, looking at her. "I'm not sure if he would, but I'm willing to ask."

She smiles. "No. Besides, Harlin doesn't really strike fear into the hearts of men, if you know what I mean. He's more of a lover than a fighter."

I smile. "True."

Sarah exhales, tugging on the ends of her hair. "I wish your powers worked for me and not dead strangers."

"You make me sound like a superhero."

"Maybe you are. And your secret identity is Charlotte Cassidy—fashion victim. You're like a hot Peter Parker."

I laugh, but inside I'm miserable. I want the Need to work for her. For my family. Monroe called this a blessing, but it feels more like a curse.

Sarah wraps her arms around herself and stands up. "The worst part is," she says, "I thought he liked me. I thought today he'd sit next to me at lunch, carry my books—all that clichéd crap." Her tears brim over just as I jump up to give her a hug.

"I'm going to knee his balls so hard when I see him," I murmur into her shoulder.

Sarah straightens and wipes at the mascara under her eyes. "I'm fine," she says. "That won't be necessary."

"No. It really is. He can't do that to—" A sly smile stretches across Sarah's lips and I feel my anxiety release a little. "What did you do?" I ask.

"Nothing." She holds up her hands innocently. "I mean, I may have mentioned to a few people that his you-know-what"—she pinches her fingers together—"was so small, it didn't really count."

I burst out laughing, totally proud and ashamed of her all at once. "Did you really?"

"He deserved it," she says, and brushes her hair over her shoulder. "Now. Are you going to come hang out with me or not? I can't go back to school today. I figured we could go hang out at my place. Daddy's in Seattle today." She grins.

"But before we go out in public . . . do you have any hats?"

I touch my stitches softly. "Does it look that bad?"

She shrugs. "If you weren't blond, it probably wouldn't be so noticable. But because you are, it looks a bit tragic. Ready?"

"Can I shower first?"

Sarah groans. "Fine, but hurry up. My driver's waiting outside and he's a total bastard when I take too long." She reaches over to grab the greasy Frankie's bag off my bed and brushes the crumbs into it. And again, I resent the Need. I resent how it controls who I can help. But no matter what it makes me do, this is my life. And I want to get back to living it.

I stand naked and stare into the full-length mirror in my bathroom, horror on my face. All of the skin on my shoulder is gone. There's no blood. No scab. Just . . . gold. A golden glow from the spot where Harlin used to kiss me. Massage me.

I fight back the tears but they leak out anyway. I don't want to believe in the Forgotten, but this, whatever it is, isn't right. It's not . . . human. I cover my mouth with my palm, trying to quiet the sobs.

This can be fixed. I'll go to Monroe and I'll demand that he fix it. He's a doctor. He won't let this happen to me. Not if I beg. I close my eyes, letting a tiny bit of calm stretch over me.

There's a knock at the door and I jump.

"Hurry up," Sarah calls. "Alex just got home from school and he's starting to piss me off out here."

"One sec," I answer automatically. When Sarah's here, I have to forget about this. I have to cover it up. I'm still Charlotte Cassidy. I'm still me.

I turn on the hot water. I can't wash where my stitches are, and I'm scared to get water on my . . . shoulder. So I reach my hand in and grab the washcloth, wetting it and then running it under my arms. I wash myself like this and then use my fingers to comb my hair, trying to work out the dried blood. When I'm finished, I turn off the water. It's not great, but it's better.

I finish up with brushing my teeth and then gather the top of my hair into a barrette to cover the stitches. Lip gloss. Earrings. I look almost normal as I slide my arms into my fleece robe, because I certainly can't walk out in a towel. Not when part of me is missing.

Quietly, I creak open the bathroom door and peer out. Down the hall I can see Sarah's school uniform, the skirt too short, as she leans against the kitchen counter, bitching at Alex. They're arguing about whether or not her bag is a knockoff. It's definitely not. Alex just likes to irritate her.

I tiptoe out and then bolt for my room, closing the door and locking it so I can get dressed. I tear through my closet, needing something thick enough to hide the light. I find a gray wool sweater and slip it over my head. Then I grab some jeans and pull them on before stuffing my feet into a pair of boots. A little overdressed for a semi-warm fall day, but it'll do.

One more glance in the mirror, and then I make my way to the kitchen. Sarah turns and sees me.

"Jesus, Charlotte. Going hiking on Mount Hood?"

Alex leans over the counter and laughs at Sarah's joke as I step out of the hallway.

"Oh, shut up," I say, and grab a piece of toast from Alex's plate.

"You're cranky," he says. "And after I let you sleep in all day. Not very nice. Besides, why were you sneaking out barefoot this morning?"

"What?" Sarah asks, glaring at me.

I stiffen. So he did notice. Well, nice job, Alex. "I think I was still half-asleep," I say. "I came back and crashed."

"So mysterious," Sarah mutters, and straightens up. "By the way, Harlin called me while you were in the shower. Wants to come meet us. But I told him we'd be at my house and he could pick you up later."

"Harlin?" I suddenly realize that I miss him. Like, ache-in-my-chest miss him.

"Uh, yeah. Harlin. You know, that guy you hook up with all the time? The misunderstood bad-boy type?" She laughs.

Alex joins in the pretend explanation. "He's hot, sort of moody. Always wears a motorcycle jacket. Any of this ringing a bell?"

I smile. "Sounds vaguely familiar." I toss the half-eaten toast down on Alex's plate as he scoffs. "Now, if you two comedians are done?"

"Great, let's go." Sarah takes me by the arm as I wave good-bye to Alex. When we're out in the hallway, Sarah turns to me. "I need your help," she says.

"With?"

"I want you to go through my closet with me. I'm looking for the perfect screw-you dress to wear to this weekend's charity ball."

"Charity ball? Glad you're going for the right reasons."

She flashes a devilish smile. "What better reason than revenge?"

CHAPTER 10

Sarah lives on the twenty-first floor of a high-rise condo next to the river. It's posh and overpriced, but then again, it's also part of her father's multimillion-dollar real estate enterprise. The minute we walk in, she drags me to her room. I asked to borrow her phone so that I could call Harlin, but Sarah said I'd have to wait until after we played dress-up. She didn't want my hormones interfering with my train of thought.

"Okay," I say, lying across the red chaise at the end of her bed. "Let's get this over with." Sarah goes into her closet—which is as big as my entire bedroom—and pulls out an armful of dresses. I groan. "Can I call Harlin now?"

"No." She puts little effort into sympathizing with me missing my boyfriend. "This?" She puts a short yellow dress against her.

"Not unless you're trying to be Big Bird."

"Hate you." She throws the yellow dress back toward her closet and starts fingering through the other garments in her arms. When I see she's properly distracted by her friends Chanel, Dior, and Dolce & Gabbana, I reach over and grab the phone off her dresser. It's already ringing by the time she looks over.

Sorry, I mouth, and then smile as I hold the phone to my ear. She sighs loudly and tosses the pile of dresses on me before going back into her closet. I laugh and lay them out on her bed.

"So you're alive?" Harlin's voice is low and very controlled. It reminds me of the way he talks to his mother. I don't like it.

"I meant to call, but—"

"I talked to Alex a hundred times this morning, but you couldn't call me back? I was worried. I thought you'd slipped into a coma or something."

"Comforting thought."

"It's not funny. You got hit by a car last night."

"Is that what happened? I couldn't remember. Thanks, Dad."

"You're lucky I'm not. I'd freaking spank you in front of your friends."

"Mmm . . ."

Harlin laughs. "Knock it off, smartass. Now where are you?"

I relax back onto the chaise, happy to hear Harlin again, the way he is with me. Sweet. Tender. "I'm at Sarah's. She's shopping in her closet for a charity dress."

"Ah. Doing her part for mankind wouldn't mean nearly as much without a fancy dress."

"Shut up, Harlin," Sarah calls from inside her closet even though she can't hear him.

"She's such a sweet girl." Harlin laughs. "Amazing manners!"

"No work today?" I ask.

"Called in. Thought I should be around to take care of you. Obviously you don't need me, though."

"Maybe I do," I say, dropping my voice. I want to see him, be near him. I feel the craving for him grow inside me. "What are you doing right now?"

"You sound really curious, Charlotte," he says, picking up on my tone. "You sure you don't want to avoid me a little longer? They say absence makes the heart grow fonder."

My lips pull into a pout. "Are you going to be mean?" I know that things must be tough for Harlin lately. I have yet to come up with a good excuse for my Needs, and I know it's making him crazy, but what can I do? I don't want to lose him. And after hearing about the Forgotten, I know I can't tell him. Not until I figure out a way to deal with it.

He exhales. "No, baby. I'm sorry for being an idiot. Yes. I'd *love* to see you. Can I come pick you up?" The familiar warmth in his voice sends tingles down my spine.

"Yes."

"I'll be there in twenty minutes."

I hang up, and just then Sarah walks out of her closet with a delicious knee-length white dress. The kind of dress that turns heads. She presses it against her. "What do you think of this one?"

"Sinful."

"Perfect!"

I wait, my head against the back of the chaise, as Sarah tries it on and pairs it with earrings and a clutch.

"Mr. Wonderful coming to pick you up?" she asks, glancing over her shoulder as she poses in front of her full-length mirror. When I smile, she rolls her eyes. "I'd disapprove of you two spending so much time together," she says, turning back to examine her reflection. "But I know he's good in bed." She grins deviously and meets my eyes in the mirror. "He is, right?"

"*So* not going there." I stand up and stretch my arms over my head, my body still sore from the accident.

"You don't have to answer," Sarah says, like it doesn't matter. "I can tell by that stupid look on your face."

"You look really hot in that dress," I say, both to change the subject and because it's true.

"I know, right?" She smiles and then strolls over to her dresser and opens the top drawer. She takes out a small shopping bag and then brings it over, holding it out to me. "For you. And don't be all, 'Oh, I can't accept it.' That pisses me off."

I feel awful. The only thing I can offer her as a friend is the Need, a way to help her. But instead it sent me to an abandoned warehouse. "I can't accept it," I repeat, mocking her voice.

She groans and shoves it into my hands. "Take it! Did you

just listen to me cry about giving a blow job?"

"Um, yeah."

"Did you judge me and call me a slut?"

"Of course not."

"Exactly." She leaves the bag in my hands. "And there aren't many friends who wouldn't have at least thought it. You didn't. That's why I love your complicated ass. Now stop being modest and open it."

"If it's a hat I'm beating you with it," I murmur. But as I reach in my hand closes on something smaller. A box.

I pull it out and stare at the jewelry box covered in maroon fabric. "Are you proposing?" I ask.

"No. You'd leave me for Harlin." She smiles. "Now shut up and look at it."

I flick open the box and my heart thumps loudly. "Earrings?" I ask when I see them. They are simple, glittering hoops, just like the ones she has on now. "They're beautiful. Thank you."

"For the charity ball," she says, like I already knew this. "You and Harlin are coming on Friday night. Did I forget to mention it?"

I narrow my eyes. "Yes. Yes, you did."

"Sorry." She shrugs. "Pick out a dress before Harlin gets here." She motions toward her closet. "Something to go with the earrings. Oh, and PS, don't wear anything trashy. Daddy hates that."

I start laughing. First, I'd never wear anything trashy. And second, because it's hilarious when she calls her stiff, stuffed-suit father Daddy. "Deal."

Sarah grabs my arm and we rummage through her designer labels, my cheeks pink from embarrassment, but also gratitude. As soon as she starts holding dresses against me, I realize that there's no way I can pull off a formal dress. Not with glowing skin. And what if the Need hits me when I'm there?

Anxiety is just about to overtake me when Sarah holds up the perfect dress. "This is it." The shimmery navy fabric is knee length and fitted without being too tight. It's paired with a matching jacket that both tones it down and adds class. Not to mention it'll cover my shoulder. I think I can actually get away with wearing it.

"Well?" Sarah asks, pushing it toward me. "Try it on."

"Uh . . ." I glance back into her room. I can't change here. I can't let her see. "It'll fit," I say. "And I should go. Harlin's probably waiting downstairs." I chew on my lip. "He's not happy with me right now."

"He's fine."

I hope she's right. "Are you sure I should borrow this?" I ask, touching the silky fabric. "Maybe I can borrow something from Mercy."

"Not that kind of event, Charlotte," she sings, folding the dress over her arm. "I'll have my driver drop it off at your place. I don't want you taking it on a motorcycle. Now, run off and catch your Romeo. But please tell him that it's *black tie*. And that means no leather."

I thank her profusely before backing away, thinking again how perfect the dress will be. But as I leave her place, I feel the questions building again. I've been putting them out of my mind, trying to be a friend. Trying to have a normal life.

I'm about to burst into tears again when I get to the outer doors and see Harlin waiting at the curb on his motorcycle. He looks over just as I see him, a soft smile on his lips. He holds out his hand to me, and again, I feel like I can breathe. I rush out to meet him.

"Not a chance," Harlin laughs as we climb off his bike in front of his apartment. He looks tired from staying out late with me, or maybe it's from worry. His dark hair is hanging near his eyes and his bristled chin has gotten scruffier. Which is actually a look that I like, so I don't mind.

"Please go with me?"

"Charlotte," he says. "Since when do you like Sarah's high-society charity events? And since when do you think I do?" He's smiling at me, his hazel eyes amused and curious.

I shrug. "I don't. But she invited us and I'll feel bad if we don't go." I squeeze his hand. "Besides, it might be cool to hang out together all dressed up."

"Will there be a band?"

"Maybe."

His dimples deepen. "So you'll save me a dance?"

"Every one of them." He watches me for a long moment before exhaling. "Okay, but I'm not shaving."

I grin. "I'm glad."

He leans forward to give me a quick kiss. "I know. By the way," he says, reaching into his pocket to take something out. "I saw this and thought of you."

"A present?" I grin and snatch it out of his hand. He's laughing, but when I look down, I gasp.

"It's pretty, right?" he asks, reaching over to brush a strand of my hair behind my ear.

"Yeah," I say without looking away. In my palm is a clear stone, and inside it is a small ivory statuette. A guardian angel.

"Figured if you're going to be out at night getting hit by cars, you might as well have some backup."

I look at him, feeling stunned. Like this is some sort of sign. But as I stare at Harlin, his mouth curved in a confident grin, I don't care about signs. I get on my tiptoes and wrap my arms around his neck, pressing my mouth to his.

We stand there, kissing in the middle of the sidewalk in front of his building. But I don't notice anyone but him. I'm taken in by the feel of him, the smell, the beauty. Harlin is like my drug—my constant need.

"I love you," I murmur.

His hands rest on my hips. "Show me," he says with a soft smile, and then pulls me inside.

Harlin's brothers are gone and we're in his room, backed against the door. He kisses at my neck as I pull at his shirt. I yank it over his head and then he's against me again, kissing me hard.

Harlin's hand slides beneath my heavy sweater as I work on undoing his belt. When he pushes my bra strap off my shoulder, I freeze.

What was I thinking? I'm missing a huge patch of skin and if Harlin sees—oh, God.

I push his hand away and shake my head. "I can't," I say, trying to catch my breath.

"What?" He doesn't seem to understand and comes back toward my mouth, kissing me.

"Stop," I say softly.

He does. Harlin's eyes are glassy with desire as he moves back, his belt nearly undone and his shirt off. "Charlotte," he says, his voice raspy, "if you're not in the mood, I understand. But if . . . things have changed." He pulls his eyebrows together as he considers his words.

Harlin is never one to be insecure, but the last few months, I've been gone a lot. I knew he'd start wondering sooner or later. This was what I was afraid of.

"My feelings haven't changed. It's nothing like that." I put my hands on his chest and then hug myself to him. "I . . . I . . ." *I'm a freak? I'm not sure I'm human anymore?* What can I say? "I have to go somewhere right now. Can we talk about this later?"

I glance up to see him looking past me, at the door. "Sure," he says with a nod. "Whenever you can pencil me in." His

106

jaw's tight and the expression on his face is cold. But I can't explain to him about my shoulder. I don't even know what it is.

"Harlin—"

"Did you really get hit by a car?"

My eyes snap to his, but he won't look at me. "What?"

"You're so secretive. Did you really get hit by a car?"

"Yes."

He swallows hard. Then he looks at me, his eyes troubled. "You're lying to me about something, Charlotte. I know you are."

I can't answer. I want to tell him everything. I'm thinking that maybe I should try. "It's not what you think," I start. "When I saw Monroe, he—"

And it's like I'm punched in the gut. A crushing pain fills my belly and I double over, falling to my knees on the floor. Harlin yells my name, but I can't answer. The room is spinning. I feel like I'm dying.

I collapse on my side, unable to get any air. I claw at my throat and feel Harlin next to me, trying to hold me. I don't know what's happening. This is new and I'm terrified.

It's not a Need.

Harlin has to open a window, get more oxygen in the room. I'm suffocating. I turn over on my side and reach my hand out, stretching for the glass across the room.

A scream gets caught in my throat. On the other side of Harlin's window, crouched down on the fire escape with her hand on the glass, is Onika—the woman in black. Her coat and boots are slick as rain starts to pour down around her. She smiles at me as she traces her gloved finger down the window. And then my vision blurs and I go dark.

"We really should stop meeting like this."

My eyelids flutter and I'm standing on the bridge near the railing where Onika's perched. It's not raining here, but the clouds cover us in gloom. "What's happening?" I ask. I clench my stomach, but before I can even think about the sickness there, it's gone.

"You passed out on the boy's floor. He's cute, by the way."

I stare at her and then look around at the empty road, the empty city. It's like we're the only living things left. She smiles as if reading my thought. With an agile movement she hops down from the railing, her boots slap on the pavement.

"Why this bridge?" she asks. "My crossover was supposed to happen off a tower in London. It was a building where I lived for a long time." She seems lost in a memory.

"I don't know what you're talking about," I say. "I'm not taking us here."

"Of course you are, love. These are your visions, not mine. This is where the *big moment* will happen!" She fakes enthusiasm and then lets the expression fade away with a smirk. "The crossover. The spreading of the light." She laughs. "Or in other words, the place where you'll die."

A shudder runs down my body and I step back from her.

"Oh, don't worry. I'm not here to hurt you." She leans against the railing, looking relaxed. "Actually, I'm here to help you."

"How?"

"Well, for starters, I can help you get your skin back."

My eyes widen. "Really?"

She nods. "We can make a deal. I have a lot of things I can teach you. You don't have to go gently into the light, sweet Charlotte. Believe me, there's no fun in that."

"You're like me? But you didn't go into the light?"

"Not exactly like you, but close enough."

Suddenly my entire world is illuminated and I feel like I'm being pulled out of my body. But when my eyes open, I'm on Harlin's floor, staring up at his terrified face.

I remember the woman in black, Onika, and search for the window. But she's gone. Harlin brushes my hair away from my face and checks me over. I hold on to him as he stays on the floor with me, wiping my tears.

"You passed out," he murmurs, reaching to slide his shirt back over his head. "I thought you stopped breathing."

"I'm okay," I say, but my throat still burns. This time the dream doesn't fade completely. I can still remember that Onika said she could save my skin. She said I didn't have to go into the light. "I think I need to see Monroe," I say.

Harlin pulls back to look at me. "Are you kidding? Charlotte, you need to go the hospital. This is serious."

"I know. But Monroe has my records. He'll know how to treat me." I stagger, trying to stand, and Harlin straightens me.

"Baby, please."

I turn and look into his eyes, see the confusion, frustration.

And I see the distrust. But this is my chance. I have to find out if Monroe knows about Onika, and I have to find her again. I have to fight the Need.

"Let's go," I say softly. Harlin stares back, but then he puts his arm around me and helps me to the door. Even now, with him angry at me, I feel protected by him. I feel him.

Harlin grabs my green jacket and as we open the front door, Jeremy is there, his key poised to unlock the door. He has a bagel in his mouth and a surprised look on his face.

"Hey," he says suspiciously as he straightens and takes the bagel from between his teeth. "You two all alone in there?"

"Don't bother with the lecture," Harlin says in a cold voice. "Charlotte's just leaving."

Jeremy nods to me, obviously uncomfortable with Harlin's response, and goes inside. And when we're out in the hall, I dare to feel something different. A chance to be normal.

CHAPTER 11

B y the time we got outside the rain had stopped and Harlin dropped me off at the clinic just before six. When I walk in, it's like Monroe's been waiting for me. He's standing in front of a busy room, patients coughing all around us. But his gaze is trained on me.

"I need to talk to you," I say, stopping in front of him. His white lab coat is wrinkled and he hasn't shaved. His eyes are unreadable.

Without a word, he turns and begins walking toward the exam room. "We'll be in the back," he says to the receptionist before asking me to join him. I suddenly wonder if he's mad at me too. Did I do something wrong? Does he know about Onika?

I get into the room and climb up on the crinkling paper of the table. Monroe goes to the counter and begins taking out instruments that I can't see from here. I just hear them clank on the metal tray.

"How's your skin?" he asks, not turning to look at me. I'm officially freaked out by his behavior. Yesterday he came to find me, and now . . . now he's acting like I'm a stranger.

"Still falling off. What's wrong?"

Monroe stops what he's doing and faces me, his lips tight. He watches me for a long minute and I recognize the expression. I've been at this clinic far too long to not know it. It's his detachment. His way of breaking bad news and shielding himself.

"Are you going to finally explain to me what the Forgotten are?" I ask. "Because I've been having a hell of a day, and I'm pretty confused." I'm feeling defiant, my heart racing in my chest. I want to know everything. He has to tell me everything.

Monroe is silent and grabs the tray before walking over and setting it on the cart next to me. Then he pulls up a stool and sits.

"Take off your sweater, please." He's so clinical. Then, as if he didn't even speak, he reaches over to grab a needle and squeezes the plunger enough to make a thick liquid leak from the tip.

"What's that?" I ask.

"It's for your skin."

My heart skips a beat. "You can fix it?"

His eyes meet mine for only a second. "Your shirt, Charlotte."

Slightly calmed, I strip down to my bra and he asks me to lay back. He pauses above me, staring down at the huge patch of gold. He smiles, but I have to look away from him. That stupid look of amazement washes over his face again and it makes me feel invisible. Like it doesn't matter that the gold is a part of *me*.

"This is a highly concentrated vitamin E extract," he murmurs, aiming the needle at the surrounding skin. "Hopefully it'll slow down the peeling process."

"Does it work?"

He pauses. "For a little while."

When I feel the first stick of the needle, I gasp. A burning fills the area, like he's injecting glue into me. "It hurts!" I hiss.

He closes his eyes for a second, composing himself as if he hates the thought of hurting me. But then he sticks the needle in another spot. "I'm sorry, sweetheart," he murmurs.

I suffer though four more injections, two needles. Each one just as painful as the one before. All the while, Monroe won't look me in the eye.

When he's done, he tells me to get dressed and goes to clean off his tray. My arm feels stiff as I slip my sweater back over my head. I feel so hurt all over. Like there's nothing about me without pain. I'm wearing out.

"Are you going to talk to me?" I ask finally, ready to scream or hit him. "I need to know the truth about the Forgotten. You have to help me stop this."

"I've told you the truth," he says quietly. "And I can only help your symptoms. The rest is out of my hands."

The weight of the world seems to fall on me. "I don't believe you. I know you can help. Why are you being so cold to me?"

"You're the Forgotten and I'm your Seer. I can't intervene."

"Look at me!"

He flinches and meets my eyes. And there I see his pain, his conflictedness. There I see his absolute devastation. And I know how much he cares about me.

"Don't let this happen," I plead.

Monroe reaches out to pat my hand, and then takes the tray back over to the counter. "I can't let our friendship cloud my judgment," he says. "You have to fulfill your destiny. It's the only way."

Anger gathers inside me. He's lying. "That's not what Onika says."

The tray slips from his hand, banging and vibrating onto the floor so loudly I reach up to cover my ears. My heart races from the jolt, but Monroe doesn't move. He's like a statue.

I slowly uncover my ears and stare at the back of his white lab coat. "You know her."

"She's found you," he whispers without looking at me. Slowly he walks to sit on a stool in front of me, a faraway expression on his face. He doesn't acknowledge what just happened.

Monroe looks up, gazing into my eyes. "You know, Charlotte, the first time I met someone like you, I was a child in London. When I saw the twelve-year-old girl who lived in the flat above me, I knew she was a different kind. Your kind.

"Jacqueline and I used to play in the hallways; tag, hide-and-go-seek. I was drawn to her, even though she was a few years older. It was like we needed to be around each other. She started to run off secretly and I would search for her; I had an intense desire to find her. But she was changing fast, even if neither of us knew what was happening. How she would cry." He closes his eyes.

"And then one day, she was gone. I was so overwhelmed with loss. I went to her mother, demanding to know where she'd sent her." Monroe looks at me again, his eyes wide. "But she didn't know who I was talking about. She didn't remember her."

The world tilts. "What?" A cold shiver races over my skin and I recoil in horror. I remember the way Callie and Francisco forgot me after I fulfilled their Needs. What does this mean? "How could Jacqueline's own mother not know her?"

"She was a Forgotten," he says. "Erased from the world, from the memory of the very woman who raised her. Gone from everyone except me. Her Seer."

"But . . ." My mind is running ahead, trying to comprehend what he's saying, but I can't. I don't understand.

"To the rest of the world, she was like déjà vu. A familiar feeling. That is your kind. The Forgotten will help or save someone, each time coming closer to their destiny—and then once they're done, they're gone. People forget them, pictures

115

fade out, records are gone. It's like they never existed. All that's left is this glimmer of hope in each person they've touched. Every person who has known them. They leave us with a feeling like there's something else out there. Almost like faith."

"You're saying . . . no. It's not true." I shake my head, disbelieving. I know that Mercy and Sarah would never forget me. And not Harlin. Never Harlin. "How do you know all this?"

"Let me finish," he says gently. "After Jacqueline, I began to notice things that other people didn't see. Certain people moving among us, like ghosts. And I didn't forget them like everyone else. In fact, I was drawn to their light. Soon I began to crave it. I went searching for them all over the world. When I was in Italy, I came across an old church where one of the Forgotten was a priest. He showed me text, ancient tablets dating back to the beginning. And in them was a chronicle of the Seers. I'm not the first. Hell, I'm not even the only one right now. We're scattered throughout the globe, looking for our Forgottens. We have to protect the light."

Was this why I've trusted Monroe all these years? He's a Seer and I'm some sort of ancient prophecy? Did I never have a choice?

Monroe reaches into the inside pocket of his coat and pulls out a small leather medical journal. He holds it up to me. "I started documenting my time as a Seer, just like the ones before me, as a way to preserve the short lives of the Forgotten—a chronicle of their time on Earth."

I want to rip it from his hands and find out everything he

knows. But I dig my fingers into the paper of the table and let him continue.

"And after years of studying, I found that every Forgotten has a limited life span. Some start as children, like Jacqueline, others not until they're adults. I've even met a few in a senior center, doing their deeds before fading. They just appear—no life before, yet the universe compensates for that, gives them an identity. And then light grows inside the body until it's compelled to help. It will brighten until you're finally set free." He stops, his hand shaking as he holds the book. He opens it, turning toward the middle.

"No life before," I repeat. "So it wasn't post-traumatic stress that took my memories."

"No. I only told you that so you wouldn't be frightened, sweetheart. I've tried to do the best I can for you. I care about you, Charlotte. I've loved all of the Forgotten in some way. Especially you. But I always lose." His face breaks a little before he straightens it. "I can't stop your crossover. I'm so sorry."

"No." I shake my head. It's too horrible to comprehend.

Monroe blows out a breath and I see the doctor side of him take over again. It's his defense mechanism. "As your skin peels, I can apply a compound, enough to hide you in normal circumstances. But your time is short. Maybe a few weeks?" He pauses. "Maybe less."

The pain in my chest is going to kill me and I lie on the exam table and curl up. I feel like a child. I'm scared and alone, just like I was in the moments before Mercy found me in the hospital. Inside I know that Monroe is telling me the truth, but it hurts too much to believe. I can't let myself believe him. "My family won't forget me," I murmur.

"That's the hardest part," he says, tilting his head to look at me. "You will slowly be erased from their memories until there are none left. Eventually they won't even remember having met you. That's why I'm here. Because even when everyone else forgets you, I'll still be here. I'll guide you until the end, just like I did for the others."

"I don't want to end." I climb down from the table. "You have to fix this. Otherwise I'll ask Onika. She says there's a way to—"

Monroe stands up and grabs me hard by the shoulder. "You stay away from that beast," he hisses. "Don't you listen to a word her forked tongue spews."

"What?" He's hurting me, but the look of terror on his face has me shaken. "But she said—"

Suddenly there's a tug in my gut, but when I try to ignore it, it becomes an intense pain. I wince, pulling away from Monroe to lean back over the table. "It's the Need."

"The Need?" he whispers to himself, as if he likes the term.

"Make it stop," I growl, pushing my forehead down into the table as I continue to writhe. "Make it stop."

He's at my ear. "Don't fight it. It'll destroy you."

"It's destroying me anyway!" There's another painful turn, this time at my side, and I scream.

I'm compelled to leave. My body feels like it's on fire and

I squeeze my eyes shut, trying to stop myself from going. I still have so many questions. But I can't stay. The Need won't let me.

I straighten up as best I can and back away. I feel like a puppet, only instead of strings, I'm guided by ribbons of heat that tear through my flesh. There's a file set in the plastic basket on the back of the door and I have to reach for it.

Monroe says nothing as I yank the folder out and flip it open, the pages blurring in front of me. I'm pushing through the papers, waiting for something to come into focus. And then it does. It's the name of a pharmacy. Dell's Drugs. Dell's is just a block or two away, and all at once I know that someone is there waiting for me. Waiting right now.

My feelings fade but I don't move. I don't want to go. "What happens if I don't fulfill the Need?" I ask without turning around.

"You must. It's your destiny."

"What happens if I don't?" I ask again louder.

"Then the light will be lost. The people you're meant to save will lose hope because they won't feel that love. That acceptance."

I laugh bitterly, the cruelty of it too much. "So I just have to sacrifice myself? Dissolve?" My hand clasps the doorknob. My body is pulling me out the door, but I have to hear him out. I want him to tell me I don't have to go.

Monroe walks over and hugs me, resting his cheek on the top of my head. But I don't squeeze back. Instead I feel the binding of his journal in his coat pocket.

"It's truly beautiful," he whispers. "A burst of bright light like nothing you can imagine. It'll fill the world with a moment of unconditional love. Everyone you've touched will have peace."

"And then I'm gone?" I slowly snake my fingers into his outside pocket and wrap them around the leather-bound pages. It feels like old skin.

"Released back into the universe," he murmurs. "Sent home."

"Well," I say to him, sliding the journal under my sweater before backing up. I meet his eyes. "I think that destiny sucks."

Without waiting for a reply, I slip out of the exam room and through the white-floored lobby. I'll find a way to beat this. But right now I have somewhere else I need to be.

CHAPTER 12

Dell's Drugs is on the bottom floor of an apartment building on the corner of Eighteenth Street. It's in an old brick structure, but inside, Dell's is as antiseptic as can be. White walls, white tiled floors—even the shelves are white. As I enter, the Need continues to burn me. Tearing me up from the inside.

The cashier glances at me, but doesn't say anything. She pops her gum and goes back to reading the latest issue of *Seventeen*. Toward the back I see the sign for the pharmacy and a rush of air blows past me. I reach out to hold on to the nearest shelf.

"You okay?" I hear. I nod and look up, seeing the cashier staring at me. She shrugs and flips the page of her magazine.

I reach in my pocket and touch the journal, comforted by its existence. Monroe said he's been documenting the Forgotten. If Onika's like me, she must be in here. And it'll say how she fought the crossover.

I slowly start to make my way down the aisle, feeling the pain increase as I go, but wanting to get out of the cashier's line of vision. There is a searing pain in my shoulder, radiating under my arm and starting across my chest. I know it's my skin. I wonder if the injection Monroe gave me can keep it from peeling off.

Holding on to a cool metal shelf, I look ahead to the small waiting area next to the pharmacy counter. Sitting in the chairs is an old couple—the woman looking very frail. And next to them a mother, holding a wiggling toddler on her lap.

Nothing about them strikes me, so I walk ahead, looking for my Need. Strong cramps turn my gut and I stumble a few more steps until I can see the counter.

And then a rush of wind goes through me. Standing there is the pharmacist. He's maybe thirty, thinning dark hair, glasses. He looks completely average until a violent pain in my head starts to blot out my vision. And again, I am blind. Then in my mind, I see him.

Miles Rodan is in bed, moving beneath the sheets. The red-haired woman with him isn't his wife. The scene changes and Miles is home, a pretty dark-haired woman is yelling at him, threatening to leave. Planning to take the kids. He begs her to stay, but she doesn't. She knows he was having an affair.

The vision changes and I feel sorrow, as if I am Miles. I'm sitting alone in the kitchen, bottles of medication in front of me. I'm filled with despair and the most isolating loneliness I've ever known. It's like drowning in a deep, dark lake.

And then I see Miles again. He pops a few pills into his mouth and chases it with a sip of Jack Daniels. His wife is gone, and so is the mistress. Everyone's miserable. He holds the prescription bottle in his hand and shakes out a few more pills. It's all his fault. It feels like my fault. He takes a few more. . . .

I'm pushed as my eyes fly open and I move toward his light. I hear the shuffle of the old lady who was in front of me in line, but I can't see her. I can only see Miles, glowing from behind the counter. Sweat begins to gather on my forehead and above my lip. He has the medication now. Tonight he's going to kill himself.

Invisible vines try pulling me forward, but I hold my spot in line, not wanting to draw attention. Behind the counter, Miles's light pulsates. If I don't stop him he'll be dead by the end of the night.

The woman in front of me turns around and asks if I'm okay and it takes all of my concentration to tell her in a nearly normal voice that I am. But when she looks away, I cover my face with my hands. I don't want this. Every Need makes me worse—brings me closer to disappearing forever.

Miles calls for the next person in line and the woman shuffles ahead. They talk as his fingers click on the computer, but their voices sound far away. Behind my eyes I can see Miles.

How he'll gag from the pills. How he'll mix them with alcohol for a lethal combination. And how he'll lie crying on his bed, twisting in agony before he dies.

"Next."

I hear it but I don't move. I almost can't. But the Need is there, forcing me to do this. I gasp and step forward, keeping my eyes toward the ground.

"How can I help you?" Miles asks, but his tone is cautious. I wonder if I look like an addict. With incredible effort I lift my gaze and stare at him, his light.

"Don't do it," I murmur. A new pain burns into my back and I wonder if the skin there is peeling off. It makes me whimper.

"Excuse me?" Miles says. "Look, do I need to call the cops?"

Cops? My fists ball up and I feel angry. The Need puts me in these situations, makes me do these things. I'm not a drug addict and I'm not the one planning to kill myself tonight. So he can save his judgments for somebody else. Somebody who's not melting away because she has to help him.

I lean in, my mouth tight. "I know what you're planning to do, Miles. I know about you and Gillian. And about the pills you have stuffed in your pocket."

And suddenly, unlike my usual Needs, who move away, staring and freaking out, Miles reaches to grab my arm and pulls me toward him. He twists my wrist at an odd angle and I fear he's going to snap it as he hisses in my ear.

"Was it you? Are you the one who told my wife?"

"Let go," I say, my head swimming, trying to find the words that'll get through to him. "You need help."

He drops my hand and steps back from me. His features are tense, scared. "Get out of here," he says. But nothing has changed and I know I can't leave yet.

"Please," I start to say, when a new person walks into my line of sight. She's illuminated slightly, just enough so that I can see her. The redhead from my vision. She's working in between the rows of pills, a clipboard in her hand. She glances at me and I gape at her in surprise.

"Get out," Miles says again, more forcefully.

"Gillian," I call. My Need zooms in. My knowledge of Miles fades away and I see that Gillian doesn't know what he's planning to do. She thought she was doing what was right by breaking it off with him. She was trying to protect his family.

"Yes?" she asks, stepping toward me.

"Don't," Miles orders, waving her away. But she's watching me, like she's sensed something was wrong all along.

"Gillian," I say, outstretching my hand to her. "He has pills in his pocket that he's planning to take tonight. He's going to take all of them!"

Miles shouts that I'm crazy, that he's calling the police, but Gillian looks at the back of his white coat. When she glances at me, I see the widening of her eyes and I'm sure they're glazing over with the knowledge. She's listening to me.

"Miles?" she asks. She knew something was off. She's felt suspicious because while she was taking stock, she'd noticed the missing pill bottle. The light around her starts to fade and my sight returns.

Miles turns to glare at her, the phone at his ear. "She's some psycho, Gill," he says. "Probably a junkie. Let me handle it."

"Do you have pills in your pocket?" she asks, her voice weak. Just then another pharmacy worker comes over, catching the end of the conversation.

Gillian touches her lips like she's figured it out. The man she had loved was going to kill himself tonight. Partly because of her. The other pharmacist takes the phone from Miles and begins asking him questions.

Gillian looks up at me and I expect a thank-you. But as I stand in front of her, I watch the recognition drain away.

"Sorry, miss," she says to me. "We have a situation. You'll have to come back later."

Suddenly the tension releases and I'm struck by a wave of euphoria. My eyes roll back in my head for a second and I stumble over to clutch on to a shelf of decongestants. And then just as quickly, I'm exhausted, wiped out. I glance up again to see Miles with his head in his hands. Gillian is wiping her eyes while the other pharmacist is on the phone. I saved him. The Need saved him.

But it hadn't taken long for Gillian to forget me, and that bothers me. Is it getting worse, or am I just noticing it more? I close my eyes and wait for the room to stop spinning. It feels like I'm missing more skin, but I don't have the strength to look. When I feel steady enough, I move down the aisle.

There's a tingling on the back of my neck, like someone is staring at me. Uncomfortable, I turn toward the waiting area. Onika's there. Any relief I'd felt is gone, replaced with fear. Monroe had called her a *beast*.

She smiles as she sits next to the woman with the squirming toddler. Onika's long hair cascades over her shoulder onto the fabric of her black jacket, effortlessly beautiful.

The child next to her lets out a harsh squeal as he tries to break free of his mother. Onika flinches and looks sideways at the toddler, her eyes seeming covered in shadows. I see her dark red lips move, murmuring something I can't hear. I'm frozen in place, watching her.

The child suddenly turns to her, eyes wide. Onika stops whispering and glances back at me, grinning again.

Still in his mother's arms, the toddler starts to whimper and clutches on to her before resting his head on her shoulder. The mother pats his back and says something like, "Oh, see. That's my big boy." But it's obvious that the kid is scared. That whatever Onika said—or did—to him has frightened him into silence.

Sickness starts to churn inside me. Onika stands, flicking out her gloved hand in a quick gesture, and the pain is gone.

"God, Charlotte. You look like hell," she says as she walks toward me.

"Monroe told me not to talk to you." I take a step back from her. She looks offended.

"Why? Because I'm trying to help you?" She groans. "He

is nothing if not predictable." She reaches out to take my arm and leads me into the aisle, where we're hidden by shelves of feminine hygiene products. She crosses her arms over her chest. "Monroe Swift is a liar, and the sooner you realize that, the better off you'll be."

"He said you were lying about being able to help me." My heart is racing even though I don't feel scared anymore. It's like the fear ran out of me.

"Yes, love. Because he wants you to dissolve. The sooner you do, the sooner he's free."

"What? How will he be free?"

She reaches out to brush my hair back behind my ear, a mothering gesture. It puts me at ease. "Because as your Seer he's trapped in servitude. But from what I hear you're his last Forgotten. And once you're gone, he can live a normal life. And here's a secret." She leans close to my ear. "He used to be my Seer too."

She moves back, continuing to smile. "And look"—she motions over herself—"I'm still very much here."

"How?" I'm suddenly desperate. She proves it. There is a way to stop the Need.

She waggles her finger in front of me. "No, no. Not yet. You have more to show me before I can tell you all of my secrets."

"But—"

"Shh . . ." she whispers, and I'm struck silent, unable to move or talk. My thoughts don't race, my heart doesn't pound. I'm content as I stare back at her, her words fading to the back of my mind. "I'll see you soon." Onika turns and walks toward the front door of the pharmacy, but when she's halfway there she looks over her shoulder at me. "Oh, and give my love to Mercy."

I try to ask what she's talking about when there's a sudden vibration in my pocket and I yelp, jumping back, no longer mute. My breath comes out in jagged gasps as if I just woke from a nightmare. When I look up, Onika is gone.

It takes a second until I realize that the vibration is my cell phone. I pull it out and glance at the caller ID. It's Mercy.

"Hey," I say when I answer. I feel like I haven't talked to her in a million years, and right now I really want her to tell me everything is okay.

"Don't you 'hey' me, Charlotte. You better be getting your little butt home and to bed. A car accident? And nobody calls me? Tell Monroe he's gonna be hearing from me later."

"It's not his fault," I try to say, but then realize that I won't win the discussion. Mercy's pretty good at standing her ground. "I'm on my way home right now."

"You've got ten minutes before I come and get you myself. And then you'll be sorry." She hangs up and I smile a little. Mercy's idea of sorry was scolding me for an hour and taking away my phone, only to bake something delicious because she felt guilty.

I push my phone back into my pocket, feeling normal for a minute before the day's events flood back into me. Forgotten. Onika. The journal. Dread grips me—an overwhelming dread that threatens to drown me—until my hand closes around something smooth inside my pocket. It's the guardian angel that Harlin gave me. It comforts me.

There's a jingle of the front door of Dell's as a police officer walks by me toward the back counter. I feel okay with what happened here, because someone was saved today. That's a good thing. I know it's good.

But even that doesn't shake me from the horror that's become my life. There's nothing worse than being forgotten. Like I never existed. I straighten and begin walking toward the street, feeling determined. Because I know, no matter what Monroe says will happen, I'm going to want to stop the Need. Even if I have to use Onika's help. I want to live.

When I open my apartment door, I'm immediately assaulted with Mercy's hugs and questions. About every other word is Spanish as she demands to know how a car had hit me, how many stitches I'd gotten, and why I didn't call her. I see both Alex and Georgia at the table, eating dinner, and I wave to them. Alex salutes me and Georgia goes back to twisting strands of spaghetti on her fork. I'm sad that she doesn't seem happier to see me. I thought we'd bonded last night. That maybe we could be family now.

"I'm sorry," I say over and over to Mercy. "I didn't want to bother you at work."

"Where did it happen? Who was driving? I'm very upset with you, Charlotte. You were supposed to be home."

I look over and see Alex widen his eyes like he knows I'm in trouble. He's the one who told her, I'm sure.

"I'm hungry," I whine, motioning toward the table. Guilt crosses Mercy's face.

"Okay. Enough third degree. For now," she warns. "Sit down and have something to eat." She puts her arm around me and leads me over; checking my stitches to make sure Monroe did a good job. She says he did.

"Looks delicious," I say, happy to put a pile of spaghetti on my plate. I'm starving after the pharmacy incident. Too hungry to think of anything else. I immediately begin to shove pasta into my mouth, my other hand grabbing bread. It's a hunger that I can't fill. I feel bottomless.

"Still can't believe the clinic didn't call me," Mercy mumbles. "Or one of my *children*." She snatches the grated cheese from Alex as he's shaking it over his plate, and gives him an annoyed look.

"Don't blame me!" he says. "I didn't know she was out running the streets. It's not like she called me, either. I didn't even see her yesterday."

"Whatever," I say to him. "I heard you and Georgia checking out my stitches while I was on the couch."

Georgia glances up, a puzzled look on her face, but she continues to eat.

"Georgia," Mercy says, slapping her hand dramatically on the table. "You told me you haven't talked to her all week."

"I told her about the accident," I say. "And we talked about other things." I smile at Georgia as she takes a drink, letting her know that I won't tell about her mother or her scar. Like it's a secret just between us. Instead, Georgia coughs on a sip of her iced tea.

"Did not," she snaps. "I don't know what you're talking about. I haven't seen you in days. Don't drag me into your lies, Charlotte."

"Georgia!" Mercy scolds.

I nearly drop my fork. "What?" I murmur.

She's staring at me, looking completely pissed off. "I didn't even know you were hurt until Mercy came in all yelling about it."

"Uh-oh, Ma," Alex interrupts. "I think Charlotte might be using that wacky tabacky." He laughs like this a joke. Like my life isn't ending.

"I heard you last night," I say to him, feeling desperate. "You don't remember?"

"Charlotte, I didn't see you until I found you in your room this morning. There you were with blood in your hair."

"You had blood in your hair?" Mercy asks, touching her chest in concern. "Poor thing. I wish you had called me. You know I would have taken care of you."

But her voice is a million miles away. My eyes tear up as I stare between Alex and Georgia, realizing that they don't remember. They don't even remember seeing me. The memories are blotting out.

"Are you crying?" Alex asks incredulously. "What the—"

"Excuse me," I say, pushing back in my chair and tossing my napkin onto the table. I run for my room as Mercy calls after me, but I don't wait. I burst into my room and collapse on the bed.

I want it to stop. I need it to stop. I sob into my hands, praying, wishing, making deals with whoever will listen. My head pulses with each tear and my bruised thighs still ache, but it doesn't matter. Nothing will matter if I don't find a way to stop the Needs.

Because before long, no one will even care. They won't even remember me.

CHAPTER 13

I must have fallen asleep because when I wake up, the room is dark and quiet. No light outside my window, no clinking of dishes beyond the door.

My eyes search for the alarm clock, and when I find it, I see that it's three a.m. I'm tired, but I move to switch on the light. My day is a blur, a pile of unsorted emotions.

I try to swallow, my throat dry, when I see my coat folded over the edge of my bed. Mercy must have brought it in here after dinner.

I jump out of bed and search the pockets frantically. When my fingers close around the journal, I exhale, relieved. But soon that relief is replaced with anxiety. A frightened curiosity.

For years I've watched Monroe take notes in this small bound book, never really wondering why. But now I know that it could hold the key to my survival. And that he had it all along.

Taking the book into bed with me, I ease under the covers, holding it tight. I turn to the first page and begin to read.

12/5

Lourdes never showed up for our appointment. When I went to speak with her husband, he didn't remember her. Looking over my last journal, I can see the pattern. It seems once the Forgotten get toward the end of their life span, they become less memorable. Almost like the people who they touch have short-term memory loss. And their families start to forget little things, little bits of their lives, until they are erased entirely.

During our last visit, Lourdes told me that her husband didn't remember their honeymoon. He claimed that they never had one. She pressed him and tried to find the pictures to prove it, but they were gone. Instead her husband said they stayed home, although he couldn't remember exactly what they did. So she stopped going back to her house. She gave up.

The memories will become foggy—like the person never existed. The writings, pictures . . . all gone. It seems that all that's left behind is space. Empty spaces or the tricks that the mind uses to fill the time. Filling it with familiar things, almost like how you can drive home without ever having to think of where to turn.

Lourdes's husband asked me if I was some kind of freak when I showed up at their place. He didn't remember his wife, and I'm just glad they didn't have children. I'll miss her.

3/8

Today I went to see Theresa but she was gone. Her room at the hospital was empty and the nurse couldn't remember ever having treated her. Again, I'm the only one to hold her memories, and it hurts. She was my friend. I feel lost without her.

She never had children, which is another common thread among her kind. They do not reproduce. There's no one to remember them but me. And eventually they all withdraw from society when the forgetting becomes too painful, until they disappear from it completely.

I've asked myself a million times, Why me? Why am I the one who sees them? From all of my research with religions and early societies, I've learned that the other Seers throughout history were thought to be clairvoyant, or ill. But I'm no fortune-teller. I'm cursed with knowing ghosts. I wish I could meet another Seer, but they're hard to find. I have yet to meet someone else like me, even though I know from the scriptures that they're out there. Searching for their lights to guide. I'm waiting for my last Forgotten. And when he or she comes, the light will be different. Stronger. It will let me go. I feel like I've been waiting my whole life to be free of this.

I start flipping through the pages, trying to find out where I come in. I find passages about the Forgotten crossing over, the brilliant burst of light as they fall from some high place so that they can scatter. How it's the *most beautiful thing in the world.* But I'm starting to hate the word "beautiful." There's nothing beautiful about me. And then I find a page that makes me gasp.

8/12

I met her today. Onika Nowak was standing in front of the college when I walked by. As she and I exchanged a glance, a woman in an old Chevy drove up and yelled to her in Russian. She pretended to not hear the woman, but I suspect it's her mother. I could tell by the way she ignored her. It was kind of cute. Onika is in my class and she's beautiful and blond, like nothing I've ever seen before. She is

The page stops, likes he's cut off mid-sentence. Like something important had happened, stopping him. I read over the entry again. And then again.

A memory floods back and I can hear Onika tell me that Monroe used to be her Seer. "Oh my God," I murmur. She didn't cross over. She's still here, which means that Monroe *does* know how to stop this. I start shaking with the first real possibility of it.

My heart pounds wildly in my chest as I turn the page.

8/24

Onika and I are going out tonight. She said she'd eat Italian, Thai, or anything that's not Russian. I think it's because of her mother. I don't blame her. Onika makes me feel normal again. I think I'm falling in love with her.

From there, the journal jumps wildly. Some pages are blank. Some are just one-sentence bits of nonsense. By the next full entry, nearly three months had passed.

11/30

It's happening. I don't know how I didn't see it sooner, how I didn't know she was a Forgotten. I can't lose her like the others. I have to stop this.

My eyes widen. Monroe was so insistent that there was no cure, but he had tried for Onika. It worked, so why not for me? Doesn't he care about me, too?

The entries turn into formulas, medication combinations, and lists of names. It's becoming frantic, impersonal. I start blazing through the pages, looking for the result.

1/6

She found me today in the lab. I injected her with vitamin E and collagen. She said it hurts but that it's working and her skin

is staying on. But I think she's lying to me, and I think she's been lying a lot.

She's holding back the impulses. I've restrained her the last few times, and it seems to pass, but only with a lot of pain. It's hard to watch. But she's going to classes again, trying to be really present in life, which is completely the opposite of how the other Forgotten let their lives go. But something's wrong. She's acting different. But I don't know what to do. She tells me to trust her.

I scan the next few entries, each one becoming more desperate. Monroe isn't saying what's happening to Onika, but with each new page, his notes become more clinical. And then, they stop all together. A chunk of about fifteen pages has been torn out, only jagged edges left behind.

What happened to her? I turn back to the beginning to look again for clues.

"Charlotte?"

I jump, startled by my name being called from the kitchen. What? What time—? I glance at the clock and feel completely disoriented. School starts in thirty minutes but it seems that only seconds ago it was nighttime. Behind my bedroom window, the sun is peeking out over Portland. I pick up my phone from the side table and see that I've missed four calls. All from Sarah.

I lost a huge piece of time and I want to keep reading, try to figure out the formulas. If anything worked. But just then, I get a text from Sarah.

Need you today. Are you alive?

I look at the journal in my lap, then back at my phone. The smell of bacon is wafting into my room, but I don't want to get up yet.

Not coming today, I text back.

I'm about to go back to the journal when my bedroom door swings open, scaring the hell out of me.

"Hey," Alex says, standing there and buttoning his wool coat. "Mercy's looking for you. You're going to be late."

"But . . ." My phone vibrates. I don't look at it because I know Sarah's going to cuss me out, or worse, be nice. Sarah uses sweetness as a weapon. The journal is in my lap and I look at Alex.

"That dinner was intense last night, right?" he asks. "I thought Georgia was going to cut you."

"Thanks for having my back," I murmur.

He laughs. "I would have gladly backed you up, but I had no idea what you were talking about. I didn't know you got hit by a car. Not until the next day when I came in here to steal your moisturizer. You need to lay off the weed, sister."

He's forgotten seeing me that night. What if he forgets everything? I'm suddenly scared of losing him. "Alex?" I ask, needing some assurance. "Remember that time when we were kids and I accidentally tripped you and you fell down the stairs? You needed like eight stitches in your arm?"

"Yeah, Charlotte. Still have the scar."

I laugh out loud, thankful. So thankful that he can remember. "Sorry about that."

"Sure you are. Now are you getting up or not? Mercy made you breakfast."

Then I realize that if I stay in this room, I won't be building new memories. I'll let myself fade away. I can't fight the Need yet, but I can fight against being forgotten. Maybe that's what Onika did. Monroe did write that she started going to classes again.

And if I go through the motions—school, going out—I'll be reinforcing my existence. They *can't* forget me if I never leave.

"I'm getting up right now," I say seriously to Alex. He furrows his brow, possibly confused by the Terminator tone in my voice.

But at least it's something for him to remember.

I grab my robe off the back of my desk chair and wander out into the hallway after Alex leaves. My stomach growls from the smell of eggs and bacon. When I get to the kitchen, I see Mercy, setting a plate on the counter and scooping eggs out of a pan when she looks up to see me.

"Morning, honey," she says with a sad smile. "Are you feeling better today? Monroe called earlier and said you might be a little confused because of your head injury." She tsks, and comes to check on my stitches again.

"He called here?" Somehow it bothers me that he's checking on me. As if he's trying to control me. I don't like it.

141

"What else did he say?" I ask, putting a forkful of food into my mouth.

"That you were very upset last time he saw you. He didn't say why. . . ." She pauses. "Are you having problems with Harlin, honey?"

"No." I resent that Monroe would even put that idea into Mercy's mind, which I'm sure he did. What better way to explain my depression than a breakup? I want to call him right now and tell him to drop dead, but I know I don't have time for that. I don't have time for Monroe, he'll remember me no matter what. Right now I just have to have a normal day. Reaffirm my existence. I have to *live* if I want to be remembered.

"Harlin and I are perfect," I say, even though that may not be exactly true. But I plan to fix that. I plan to be the best girlfriend ever.

"I'm glad. He's sweet." Mercy sits down across from me and sips from her coffee. I watch her, pain aching inside me. Mercy is the only mother I've ever known. What if she forgets me? What will I do without my mother?

"By the way," she says, putting another piece of bacon on my plate, "I thought we could go shopping later. Maybe for shoes? I'm tired of seeing you in those scuffed-up thrift-store finds."

"Oh no. I'm not walking around in chunky heels or strapless leg breakers."

"Fashion is your friend, Charlotte."

"You sound like Sarah."

Mercy playfully rolls her eyes. "Then God help me." We

sit quietly, both smiling as we share a meal but then suddenly, I'm struck with loss.

"I love you, Ma," I say.

She puts down her coffee cup and beams at me, looking completely surprised. "I love you, too." Her eyes fill up with tears. "You're still my little girl, no matter how old you get." She smiles and wipes quickly to keep from smudging her black eyeliner.

And I try to smile back, but I'm crying too. Because unless I can stop this, I won't be her little girl anymore. I'll be no one.

Sarah is waiting for me on the stairs of St. Vincent's Academy, tapping her black leather shoe. It's nice seeing her like that, annoyed. It means things are still the same.

"Morning," I say, jogging up to meet her.

"*Morning?* What the hell is with the cheerful? And where's my latte?" She glances at her watch because I'm close to twenty minutes late, which is why I didn't make the usual coffee stop.

"At least I'm here today, right?" I bat my eyelashes as she grabs me by the elbow and walks me into school.

The halls of St. Vincent's smell like furniture polish and incense. The ceilings are tall, and dark wood floors stretch ahead of us.

"Here's the current situation," Sarah says, applying lip gloss as we walk. "Seth heard I made an unflattering comment about his . . . anatomy and physiology, and he's not pleased." She grins anyway. "And now he wants to meet me at lunch."

I turn to her. "You are not meeting him."

"I know I shouldn't," she says. "But I'm kind of curious, you know? I mean, he could bitch me out anytime, but he wants to meet outside in the courtyard. Alone. I think he feels bad."

I can't decide if I'm mishearing her or if she's stupid. "Sarah, he told everyone that you—"

"I know, thanks for reminding me." She scrunches her nose and shakes her head. Out of the corner of my eye I see someone point. I look over to see Carver Braun and his buddies snickering as we pass. I take the opportunity to flip him off and then go back to Sarah.

"Look," I say. "I just can't understand why you'd put yourself through it. I mean, it's not like you're desperate for a date. You could have anyone you want." The bell overhead rings loudly and I glance up at it before looking at Sarah. When I do, she's staring at me.

"Really?" she asks. "Name one."

I run through the student body in my head when I realize . . . there is no one. Sarah has dated most of the normal, a few of the not-so-normal, and all of the bad boys. She might have to start looking at the community college.

"Not all of us have found the *guy*, Charlotte," she murmurs, and reaches to adjust the strap of her backpack. I have a guilty feeling, one that occasionally comes when it's obvious that Harlin and I aren't like everyone else.

I don't respond; just start walking toward my class and leave her behind me, not sure how I can make it right.

"Charlotte," she calls, like she's ready to apologize. "Meet me before lunch!" she adds just as I turn the corner into physics class.

Ow. I slam face-first into a muscular chest, dropping my bag off my shoulder. "That hurt," I say, touching my nose and then glancing at my fingers to make sure it's not bleeding. There's a husky chuckle and I look up to see Brandon Whaler, resident tool.

"Sorry about that, Charlotte," he says. "You should have aimed your face a little lower. You know, like your friend."

I narrow my eyes, my hands balling into fists at my side. "Brandon, you're just jealous because you know that Sarah would never get within ten feet of your shriveled, little—"

And suddenly it strikes. My vision blurs, my skin catches fire, Brandon is gone. Only this is different from the Need. This is something else.

"You okay?" I hear, but can't respond. It's like I don't have a mouth. It's like I'm not here.

I'm on the bridge, the night dark and starless around me. It starts to rain and I can feel the splatters on my skin, but when I look down, there is nothing. No rain. No skin. Just glowing light.

I search for Onika, knowing that she's always here waiting for me. Then from the other side of the bridge someone is running toward me. The wind is strong and it's then that I notice where I am, standing on the guardrail, holding on to the cables. What am I doing here? Am I going to jump?

"Charlotte!"

I look up but I can't see who it is. They're too far away, their voice muffled by the storm. But next to me there's a laugh. "Beautiful night, huh?"

"What's happening?" I ask, turning toward Onika. "Why am I here?"

She stands up on the railing, balancing effortlessly even in high-heeled boots. "It's easier to find you this way—in your visions. Although it was nice to see you in the pharmacy. Too bad about Miles, though. He's been wanting to kill himself for a long while."

In the distance I can still see a figure coming toward me and I'm frightened. I don't know what to think anymore.

"So here's my offer," Onika says, reaching over to take my chin and turn me toward her, away from the approaching person. Up close, her beautiful porcelain skin has a tiny crack along her cheekbone. I blink quickly, alarmed by it. "You stay on Earth with me," she says, "and I'll give you everything you want."

"How? How did you keep from bursting into light?"

Her icy blue eyes narrow. "It wasn't easy. And it's not for everyone. In fact, I'm not even sure you're up for it. But I've been searching for other Forgotten and they were too weak. But you're more like me. And wouldn't it be nice if that meant you didn't have to dissolve?"

"What do I have to do?" The person coming across the bridge is calling for me again, and I see Onika look toward

146

them, her delicate jaw clenching. When she turns back to me, she tries to smile. The crack in her skin spreads slowly like a spiderweb.

"I'll let you know when the time is right. I'm just happy to hear you're game. Now . . ." She lets go of my chin and flips up the hood of her jacket. "It's time for you to go. But first, a little taste of how *blessed* you'll feel if you go into the light."

And just then she rams her palms into my chest and sends me flying backward off the bridge. I feel myself falling, pain shredding my skin as I scream. I scream until my voice breaks and I squeeze my eyes shut as I wait for the imminent smack against the water. Then suddenly I feel myself being pulled out of my vision.

I open my eyes and Brandon is shaking me, telling me to stop screaming. I hear a loud noise in my ears but it takes a second for me to register my own shrieks. I stop, the sound still echoing in the room. When I look around, the entire class is staring at me, their mouths hanging open. Brandon seems terrified.

"Jesus, Charlotte. It was just a joke. You didn't have to go all *Exorcist* on me."

I'm shaking, every bone in my body feeling hot and out of place. When the teacher comes over and asks if I want to go to the nurse, I say yes and leave.

I walk through the empty halls, fear creeping up my legs and down my arms and I wrap my sweater tightly around me and move a little faster. Off the bridge, that's how I'll end—having to leap, just like the people in Monroe's journal. That's what happens if I give in to the Need.

But Onika offered a deal. She has a way to stop this, even if Monroe won't. I'm just not sure if I can trust her. And her face? What happened to cause it to crack?

I shake my head, trying to stay in the moment. I'm losing so much time, time I should be living. So I decide that if that's my end, falling off a damn bridge, I'm sure as hell not going on one. I have choices still. This is my life.

CHAPTER 14

I'm still lying on the cot in the nurse's office when I hear the sound of a shoe tapping impatiently on the linoleum. I start to smile before I even open my eyes.

"Come to check on me?" I say and manage to sit up. Sarah is there, a Diet Coke in one hand and a bored expression on her face.

"Seriously?" she asks. "You let Brandon One-Brain-Cell Whaler freak you out? I'm pretty sure I kneed him in the balls last year and you gave me a behind-the-back high-five. What happened?"

"It wasn't him," I say. "I mean, yeah, he's a tool, but I don't know. I—" And I stop because I realize that I can't really explain. Visions of ghosts and falling off bridges aren't exactly normal topics of conversation. Even if that's now my life. "Never mind," I say. "I think I have a concussion."

"Probably. You look pale. Hey, you're still going to go the charity event with me, right?"

I groan.

"Pretty please? It'll be so boring without you there. I'll be your best friend."

I smile at her. "You're lucky I already know you're my best friend or my answer would have been a hell no."

The nurse clears her throat from her desk. "If you're well enough to make plans for tonight, Ms. Cassidy, I think you're okay to go back to class."

I'm a little embarrassed and nod, hopping down from the uncomfortable cot. She hands me a hall pass and I wonder if she thinks I did it all to get out of class. But I don't say anything and instead follow behind Sarah into the crowded hallway.

As I fall in step next to her, I look sideways, anxiety creeping over me. "Sarah, remember that time last summer when we drove out to the coast to see the beached whale?"

She turns, a blank expression on her face. Please, no.

"Charlotte?" she asks slowly. "Why the hell would you bring that up? You know I puked for like two hours after I smelled that thing."

I close my eyes, taking in a huge gasp of air. She remembers it.

"Getting hit by cars and screaming in class? I swear, you're getting weirder by the hour." She starts walking like she's in a hurry.

"Where are you going?" I ask as we pass the cafeteria. I'm not a fan of fish sandwiches, but right now, I'm starving. Sarah stops fast and I nearly collide into the back of her.

"I have to meet Seth, and you're coming with me."

"Ew, no way. I don't want to hear the details of your hookup."

"He won't, not with you there. But if he's willing to ask me out with you standing there, looking all judgmental, then I know he likes me."

I step back from her. "Ask you out? Sarah, he bad-mouthed you to the entire school."

"I remember," she says. "But what if—"

"No," I say, crossing my arms over my chest. "You can't go talk to him."

"Why? Did you foresee something?" She looks hopeful.

"No. But I know he's a jerk."

She looks disappointed, but then shrugs. "You're right. He is. But I still think he likes me, and now that I've put him in his place, he's ready to apologize and we can move on."

"He's an asshole."

Her face begins to darken and for a second I think she might cry. But instead, she just twitches her mouth. "You may be right," she says. "But it's all I've got." And then she walks away, leaving me alone in the middle of the hallway.

I'm just about to go double up on tater tots when a burning sensation prickles my skin. I blink slowly, the world around me fraying at the edges. Not now.

I try to turn to the cafeteria, but pain spikes through my

joints. Eventually I give in and start walking toward the back of the building.

I stare at the doors where light filters in, thinking I'm leaving the school, but at the last second a rough wind blows through me, stopping me at a wooden doorway a few feet away.

Looking it over, I see everything but the handle lose its focus. I think . . . I'm at the teachers' lounge. My skin tingles and my body is pushing me, but I don't want to open the door. I don't want to give in to the Need anymore.

But after an intense burning in my back, I reach out my hand and turn the knob. When the door opens, my sight fades. There is a glowing figure in the room, sitting at a circular table. Sister Dorothy.

If I wasn't in so much pain, I might laugh. The Need has to help a nun? It seems ironic. But I don't have time to think about it because I'm entering the room, the door closing behind me.

She looks over her shoulder at me, her features barely recognizable underneath the light. "Miss Cassidy? What are you doing in here?"

Her voice is high-pitched and alarmed, like I've broken one of the commandments of St. Vincent's: *Thou shalt not enter the teachers' lounge.* But then her life flashes before my eyes.

Suddenly, I am Dorothy Beaker. I'm in Italy backpacking with my best friend, Marjorie. We are twenty and we came to see the Vatican. Hoping to catch a glimpse of the Pope. We're waiting in the courtyard and I'm so excited. I feel like God is smiling on me.

The scene changes and Marjorie is crying as we sit in the small room at the hostel. She's pregnant. She never told me that she was having sex, and I'm offended. I'm offended that she would disgrace her religion. I tell her so. I'm breaking her heart because I am her only friend and I'm ashamed of her.

It's a year later. I'm back in Washington, living at my parents' house as I prepare for the order and there's a knock at my door. I'm annoyed. I want to keep reading but I go anyway. No one else is home.

When I open it, Marjorie is there. Her face is puffy from crying and her body looks softer, curvier after her pregnancy. She asks for my forgiveness. I tell her I'm not the one to forgive her.

I listen impatiently as she tells me how she gave her baby to the church, that she wanted to keep it but her parents wouldn't let her. She had no one. She didn't even have me.

Now she's desperate to find the baby. She asks for my help. She gets on her knees and begs for it.

In the teachers' lounge, I flick my eyes to Sister Dorothy. She's fifty-eight and small, a shadow of the woman she used to be. She stares at me, asking me questions and looking like she's going to go for the phone. But I can't hear her. I just hear Marjorie's sobs.

"Help me find her!" she cries.

But I am Dorothy and I tell her no. That she wasn't meant to have that baby. That the baby is better off with someone else. I am cruel.

As Dorothy, I resent Marjorie. She gave up both her religion and me when she sinned. So why now should I help her? She was supposed to be going into the convent with me. But now she can't.

Which is why as she cries, I shut the door and leave her.

"Sister Dorothy," I say finally, startling her. "I know what happened to Marjorie's baby."

The light around her blazes, like an overwhelming emotion just struck her. Her gray eyes turn glassy as she stares at me.

"You know Marjorie?" she murmurs, not disbelieving.

"It was a girl. Her name is Catherine." I smile a little, seeing images of the child growing up, quick snapshots of her life. She was happy.

"Heaven above," Sister Dorothy whimpers and makes the sign of the cross. She starts to pray quietly, her hands clasped in front of her.

"She has a husband and two little boys. Marjorie's grandchildren. She's always wanted to know her mother. But Marjorie passed away a few years ago. They never found each other."

"What have I done?" Sister Dorothy whispers, her eyes squeezed shut. I step forward and put my hands over her folded ones. When she looks up her eyes gaze past me, like she's not seeing me. Like she's seeing something else. Something beautiful.

"Find Catherine," I tell her. "There's an old farmhouse just outside of Vancouver. The last name is Paltz. Tell her about her mother. Tell her about Marjorie."

Sister Dorothy falls to her knees, sobbing, just as the light goes out around her and my sight returns. For the past thirty-six years Sister Dorothy has been repenting. Now she'll make it right.

I swoon and nearly fall on top of her, but I catch my footing just in time. Euphoria stretches over me and I laugh out loud, feeling so damn good.

"Can I help you?" Sister Dorothy asks sharply. She's oblivious to the tears on her cheeks as she scrambles to her feet. "You have no business being in here," she says. "New students should report to the front office. Not the teachers' lounge."

I'm stunned. She's forgotten me so quickly.

Maybe it's okay that she can't remember me, I think as I try to calm myself. It's not like Mercy or Sarah or Harlin. It's not the same. I should focus my energy on keeping *them* from forgetting.

Once I'm in the hall and the door behind me closes loudly, I try to take a deep breath. But when I reach up to scratch my nose, I see something that changes everything. There's a big patch of skin missing from my hand.

I sit alone at a table, the sleeve of my sweater pulled down to hide my right hand. With the left I'm picking through my tater tots, filling an insatiable hunger. Our usual lunch crowd is buzzing with whispers that I know are about us—Sarah's latest poor judgment and my in-class freak-out. But I don't have time for petty drama today. I need to keep building memories with the people I care about, people who love me. It's the only thing that'll keep me real.

Sarah flops down across from me, her eyes bloodshot and the tip of her nose a little red. Her freckles dot her face now that her makeup has rubbed off. She won't meet my eyes, and my heart sinks.

"Do you want to talk about it?"

"No." She opens up her backpack to take out a Ziploc baggie full of celery. After a minute of silence, she starts talking in a low voice. "We're going to have fun tonight. Just us."

"Hell yes." I don't feel all that energetic, but I can see Sarah's sadness and I'm here for her. Just like I was when her grandmother passed away last year, or when her father puts her down and makes her hate herself. I want to always be here.

I try to think of something inspiring to say. "Hey, remember that time when Rod Crowell called me fat in eighth grade?"

Sarah slowly raises her eyes, meeting mine. "You were never fat."

"I know, but he was mad that I beat him in the gym relay. Do you remember what you said to him?"

Sarah pulls her brows together, thinking hard. "No idea what you're talking about, Charlotte."

An empty feeling rolls over me. Normally, Sarah would remember that she kicked him in the leg so hard that his parents threatened to sue her father.

She'd remember telling me that no matter what anyone

says to me, my opinion of myself is the only one that matters. She's brilliant sometimes. She'd remember that.

"You really are my best friend," I say quietly, reaching out to cover her hand with mine.

She laughs and pulls back. "You're so patronizing. Of course I'm your best friend. And by the end of the day everyone's probably going to be calling you my *girlfriend*."

I try to smile. So what if she forgets little details of our relationship? She knows *me* and that's what matters. We'll just build new details. At least I'm still here with her.

I pick up a tater tot and throw it at her. "Who cares?" I say. "It's not like we have some stellar reputations to lose. The rich BJ queen and the fashion-challenged scholarship kid? We sound like a great couple."

"Imagine when the nuns call Daddy about that one."

I grin. "Oh, he'll flip. You're supposed to marry a prince or something, right?"

She sighs. "I'd almost make out with you just to spite my father."

"No thanks."

"Don't flatter yourself, Charlotte." She picks the tater out of her lap. "If you were my girlfriend, you'd have much bigger boobs."

"Hey!"

"No worries." She waves her hand. "I'm pretty sure I can't compete with Harlin."

"No," I say. "You definitely can't."

"He's good. I just know it."

"Shut up!"

"We're going to have fun tonight," she says, mostly to herself. Then she goes back to crunching her celery. But I can still see that whatever went down with Seth is bothering her. She's sad. And so am I.

CHAPTER 15

When I get back to the apartment after school, I rush to my bedroom. I rummage through my drawers until I find a pair of black gloves. Slipping them on, I look on my bed for the journal. I need to find out more about Onika.

I stare at the rumpled comforter, confused. Where is it? I left it right here. I begin yanking off the sheets, checking under the bed. But it's not here. It's gone.

I spin around, looking from the side table to the dresser, but nothing. Where is it?

"Alex?" I call out. A few seconds later he appears in my doorway, a sandwich in his hand.

"You rang?" he mocks, his hair pulled back into a ponytail.

"Did you see a journal on my bed?"

He laughs. "Since when do you keep a diary? I would have certainly read it by now."

"Did you see it or not?"

"Nope."

My heart is pounding. I hadn't finished reading it.

"Do you think Mercy would take it?" I ask.

Alex takes a big bite of his sandwich and talks through the food. "Probably. But when I got home she was walking out with Monroe."

I freeze. "What?"

"You know, the superhero Doctor Swift? He was here when I got home. Then he left with Mercy."

"Why?"

"Charlotte." He waggles his food at me. "Do you think I know? Holy hell." Alex exhales and turns to go back down the hall toward the living room.

I stand there, thinking this over. Monroe. He must have seen the journal and taken it back. Is he mad that I stole it from him? Quickly I check my phone to see if I have any missed calls, but I don't. Not from him or anyone else.

Just then the doorbell rings. I think it's Monroe and swallow hard, smoothing down my hair (because that would help?) before walking toward the door.

Alex is on the couch flipping through the stations as I walk past to the door. I brace myself for a fight with Monroe, but when I open the door and see who's standing there, a whole new feeling comes over me. Harlin.

"Hey," he says quietly. Folded over his arm is a gray cover on a hanger, holding his suit. His face is clean-shaven. His normally shaggy hair is combed smooth, sleek. Sexy.

"Hi."

In his other hand, Harlin's holding a white paper bag and holds it up for me. "It's from Frankie's. Thought maybe you'd be hungry?"

"You read my mind."

"I'm hungry too," Alex says from the couch, poking his head over the side. Harlin nods at him and reaches in the bag, pulling out a wrapped burger.

"Bacon and cheese," he calls, tossing it to him.

Alex smiles. "My man." He unwraps it and bites into it before wandering over to the kitchen. "Mmm . . ." he adds, looking over at us. "Bacon cheeseburger is so good."

I take the bag from Harlin and set it on the counter as Alex breezes past me, grabbing his jacket.

"Where are you going?" I ask.

He curls his lip. "God, nosy. Can I spend time with my own boyfriend? Oh, and tell Mercy I'll be home for dinner."

I laugh, but secretly I'm thrilled that he's leaving. There's no one else home. No one at all. I look back over to Harlin and see that he's watching me. He makes no moves toward me, just leaning casually against the door. Like he has all day. It's insanely hot. When he licks his lips, I just about die. I saunter back over toward him and wait. Alex needs to hurry up.

"Leaving now," Alex calls, as if reading my mind. "You kids be safe."

"See you later, man," Harlin calls to him as he leaves. But once he's gone, Harlin steps forward, reaches for me and pulls me into him. With his boot he kicks the door closed and brings his mouth incredibly close to mine.

"Been thinking about you all day," he whispers, his eyes closed.

"What sort of thoughts?"

"I'll show you."

"I'm guessing it doesn't involve equations or logarithms?"

"Don't even know what those words mean. Now come here." His mouth is warm against mine as he walks me backward and eases me onto the couch.

"I love you," Harlin whispers in my ear. I snuggle into him, careful to keep myself covered. To hide the gold. "I was thinking about California today," he adds, twisting strands of my hair around his finger.

I smile. "Really?"

"Mm-hmm. I'm looking at the weekend after you graduate— we could stay in Monterey for a few days, then head down to San Diego. Stay a week, maybe two."

"Sounds perfect."

"It will be. Who knows," he murmurs, moving to kiss my neck. "Maybe we won't come back."

I close my eyes, lost in this moment. Lost in him.

But it's amazing; when I'm with Harlin everything feels

right—like pieces of a puzzle that fit together to make a picture. And in the big picture, it's just him and me. Without the Need.

I stand in front of the bathroom mirror, turning from side to side. Harlin is getting dressed in my room for the charity ball while I shower. But now . . . I'm not sure I can go.

The sickness of my reflection is washing over me, and I'm too stunned to cry. I had hoped that the injections Monroe had given me would help my skin. Help it grow back. But the flesh on my shoulder is gone. There is a golden shimmer underneath, although I'm not quite sure what it is. I touch it, but there's nothing, no feeling.

I want to be normal. I just want to be a regular person with all of her skin! Standing over the sink, I start to cry, but then I remind myself that Harlin is here.

Quickly I wipe my face and then turn on the shower. The stitches in my head will get wet, but that's the least of my concerns.

The steam is all around me as I step in, letting the water hit my face, wash away the streaks of tears. I can't help thinking about my Needs. The pharmacist and how easily he would have ended his life. How he didn't change and that's why my Need switched to his mistress. That was the first time I didn't convince someone. I wonder if the Need will always find a way. If it's that strong.

Suddenly Onika's face pops into my head and it's as if she's right in front of me, standing under the water. It's washing away her makeup, and her skin underneath is gray, filled with cracks like a desert floor. She smiles.

My eyes fly open and I step back from the water, swinging out my arms. I can't see her. The steam is thick and I feel a chill, like I'm not alone. I'm gasping as I reach for the knob to turn off the water. But I'm fumbling. What's wrong with her? Why does she look like that?

My hand wraps around the faucet and turns off the water as I'm pushing past the shower curtain. But just as I step onto the white tiles of the bathroom floor, my foot slips out from underneath me. In a swift motion I fall back into the tub, grabbing the curtain for support but pulling it down with me.

When all is still, I look around the room, feeling confused. The steam is fading and I'm alone, the plastic shower curtain crumpled on top of me. She's not here.

I sit up in the tub, touching the back of my head to make sure my stitches are still in place, and I'm not bleeding. But the horror of my thoughts still clings to me.

There's no one here but me. I'm starting to go insane.

I wrap myself in my robe and peek out the door. I hear the TV blaring a football game from the living room, so I know Harlin is in there. I dash into my bedroom and lock my door.

I sit on my bed, breathing heavily. Onika's face. It was so horrible, so decayed. Is that how she looks, or is my mind playing tricks on me? I push my robe off my shoulder and stare at the gold. It's vibrant and bright.

I'm pulling my robe tight around me when I look up and see the dress from Sarah's closet hanging on the back of my door. I hadn't noticed it earlier, but realize that it must have been here all day. Sarah had it delivered.

They love me—Mercy, Sarah. Harlin. Even if they'll forget some of the memories we've created, they'll never totally forget me. Not when I'm still here, seeing them every day. Loving them back.

I walk to the closet, looking over the navy blue dress and jacket. It's pretty, and thankfully, it'll cover the gold. When I reach out to touch the fabric, I catch sight of my hand—the skin there missing and obvious without the gloves. Mercy has thick foundation in the bathroom, and I can use it to disguise the spot. Just enough to get me through the night. A night without the Need—I hope.

I don't take long to get ready, mostly because my hair dries quickly. The foundation works well enough, maybe not to close scrutiny, but enough for a charity event. A touch of lip gloss and a dash of perfume, then I make my way out to the living room.

My boyfriend is sprawled on the couch, the remote in his hand as he watches the TV intently. God. He looks good. He's wearing a black suit with a thin tie, his hair smooth. His shoes shiny. It's like he could walk the red carpet of a movie premiere. But instead he's on my couch, waiting for me. Watching *SportsCenter.*

"Miss Cassidy," he says without looking over. The fact that

he knew I was here checking him out but didn't say anything turns me on.

Sarah had texted to say she was sending a car because she didn't want us showing up on a motorcycle. I supported this idea. My hair would not hold up in the wind.

I see Harlin's lip curve with a smile as he looks sideways at me. "Come here," I say quietly. Without any hesitation, Harlin clicks off the TV and walks over, looking me up and down.

"So beautiful," he says. I grab him by the tie and pull him closer to me, kissing him hard on the mouth. I can't wait anymore. I need him.

I'm a combination of heat and desire as we stumble down the hall toward my bedroom, attached at the lips. His fingers are knotted in my hair and my hands have slipped off his fancy jacket. The town car can wait a little longer.

When we get into my room he pushes me against my door, closing it and pinning me.

"I love you," he says. "I'll always love you."

I unbutton his shirt as his hand lifts up the hem of my dress. My clothes will stay on, and that should work well. I just want to be lost here with Harlin.

Always.

CHAPTER 16

W hat the hell are you two smiling about?" Sarah asks as we climb out of the car. She's waiting on the stone front steps of the museum that her father rented out, looking kind of pissed.

"Nothing," Harlin says, putting his arm around me. "It just took me forever to get dressed."

She stares at him and then at me. "Gross. If that's code for you two just did it in the car, please spare me."

"Not the car," Harlin says with a shrug.

"Whatever." She looks me over and nods approvingly. "You look fantastic," she adds. "I really have good taste."

"You do," I agree. "What's the charity again?" Looking around the brick front, I see no reference to the cause, but there are lights swooping back and forth over the building, making sure everyone attending feels important.

"Owls, I think," she says, turning to walk inside. "No." She pauses. "The homeless."

Harlin laughs. "I can see how you got those two confused."

As we climb the steps I smile to myself and clutch Harlin's arm. I feel a million miles away from my problems, which is exactly how far from them I want to be.

When we enter the lobby, I'm blown away. Roses and red velvet drape everything: the lobby desk, the restroom signs, even the nude statue that usually greets us. The sweeping marble staircase has bouquets winding up the railing and the entire room smells like flowers. Personally I think the zillion dollars of art is enough atmosphere, but apparently the rich don't.

"I'm guessing there won't be a band," Harlin says.

"There is so," Sarah defended. "Like half the symphony is here."

"Not really the kind of band I was hoping for."

"Oh, sorry, Harlin," she says. "The Killers were already booked. Maybe next time."

"Sort of cranky today, Sarah." Harlin adjusts his tie and I'm sure he's uncomfortable in it. "Didn't you take your meds?"

"Naw." She waves him off sarcastically. "I figured I wouldn't get all crazy and jump in the fountain later if I did. And what fun is a million-dollar event if I don't disappoint my family?" She's joking but there's a ring of truth in her voice, and the fun of the moment fades. We all feel it.

Sarah clears her throat. "Charlotte?" she asks. "Will you come with me to get a drink?"

"Sure." I'm puzzled since I see the people in tuxedos walking around with trays of drinks, but I don't argue. I give Harlin a quick kiss and follow Sarah, who's already walking away.

I catch up with her and take her elbow. "You okay?" I ask.

"No. Not really." We make our way through the crowd until we're at the kitchen doors, servers rushing past us with trays of canapés.

"I'm pretty sure we can get our drinks at the bar, Sarah," I say. But she keeps going until she pushes out the back door.

We step outside onto the loading dock and Sarah starts to pace. "I wanted to be alone."

I look around. "Mission accomplished. But if you're trying to put together an art heist, count me out."

She glares at me. "Not funny."

"It's a *little* funny."

"No, really. It's not," she says. Her heels clack on the concrete as she walks back and forth in front of me. "The nuns called a little while ago."

Chills run over me and I wrap my arms around myself. Sarah is staring at the ground as she continues to pace. Now I feel guilty for the art heist joke. "What did they say?"

She pauses, and then turns to me abruptly. "That I'm setting a bad example for the underclassmen. Seems Seth told the nuns I was starting rumors about him. That I was 'desperate' for attention, so I was trying to ruin his reputation."

"He didn't!"

"Oh yes. He even said that he was concerned about my mental stability. They let my father know that little tidbit too."

"Wait. Douchebag Seth, who told everyone about *you*, went to the nuns and said you were spreading lies about him. Why would he do that? I don't—"

"When I met him at lunch he asked me to clear up the rumor about his inadequate size." She shrugs. "Which, by the way, is true. But he said his friends were making fun of him, calling him Tiny Tim." She shakes her head. "I couldn't believe that was the reason he wanted to meet with me. I thought he was going to apologize! He owes me a goddamn apology!

"So I refused. He called me a slut. I slapped him in the face. It was all very dramatic and awful, but I thought that was it. Apparently not. Instead he marched down to the main office and told Sister Mary Angela that I was out of control and sleeping around. And when I tried to get with him and he *refused*, I spread the rumor."

"Why would they believe him? That's ridiculous!"

She pauses. "Remember Brandon One-Brain-Cell Whaler? Well, he vouched for him. Said he did it with me in the locker room. He was so repentant that they didn't even suspend him."

"That lying bastard! I should have kneed him—hard—when I bumped into him in class. He's so dead."

Sarah glances up and a few tears leak from her eyes. "The closest I've ever gotten to doing it with Brandon was in seventh grade when I told him his breath smelled like Cool Ranch Doritos. He never touched me. I never let him touch me—"

Sarah breaks into sobs and I wrap my arms around her and hold her tight.

"My father's pulling me out of St. Vincent's. He says I've humiliated him."

"What?" First of all, I'm furious that the nuns would believe anything Seth or Brandon said, especially without evidence. And then to tell her father? It's so completely wrong I want to scream.

Sarah pulls back to look at me. "I guess you really aren't psychic, huh?" she says in a small voice.

And my heart breaks seeing how much pain she's in.

"I promise you I would never have let this happen if I were."

She nods. "That's too bad." She smiles sadly and I hug her again, resenting the Need. Hating the light. I should have been with her today, not with Sister Dorothy.

Sarah sniffles and rests her head on my shoulder. "The stupid thing is, I liked Seth. And more than anything, I'm . . . hurt. Why wasn't I good enough for him? How could he do this to me?"

"Oh, please. You are a million times better than that cruel bastard. He's like, bottom of the barrel, scum of the earth. And you're mostly nice. Like more than eighty percent of the time." I straighten her up and fix one of the curls that has come loose from her barrette. "And besides, you're way too hot for him anyway."

She laughs, wiping at her cheeks. "You know just what to say." Sarah dabs her finger under her eye to wipe off the mascara that's started to run. "I'm going to be a freaky home-schooled kid now."

"No, you won't," I say, taking her purse from her arm and going through it to find her compact. "And besides, home-schooled kids are not freaky."

"They have no fashion sense."

"Urban legend. Look at me, I have no fashion sense and I attend the esteemed St. Vincent's Academy for Troubled Youths."

Sarah laughs and takes the compact from my hands as I hold it out. She groans when she catches sight of her reflection.

"Now," I say. "Pull yourself together. I can't do this stuffy event without you. You have unshakable confidence and that makes you the stronger one in this friendship, so act like it."

Her smile fades. "No," she says softly. "You're the rock, Charlotte. You've held me together all these years. Still do."

"And I always will." As I say it, I want to make it true. I want to get rid of the Need and be her friend for life. I'm going to try.

Sarah pats powder under her eyes before returning the compact to her bag. When she's done, I reach out my hand to her. "Ready for that drink now?"

"Oh, I'm going to have, like, six."

"Not in front of Daddy," I warn with a mocking pout. "He's probably already cranky."

Sarah loops her arm through mine. "He's pissed all right.

Asked me if I was going to embarrass him tonight."

"You should have told him yes."

"I told him I'd already done all I could this week. But I'd try harder for the next event."

I don't laugh because I know that her father had probably said plenty to her tonight. I can still remember when we were in tenth grade and he caught us drinking in Sarah's room during a sleepover. He was furious. Told her that she disgusted him. That she'd end up a drunk just like her mother's father.

She was fourteen. But instead of crying about it, Sarah finished off the bottle of rum and I held her hair while she puked all night in her bathroom. She said he didn't love her. And I'm not sure I'd argue.

When we come back into the huge main room, Sarah excuses herself to the bar. "I'm going to see if my boobs can get me served. Then I'm going to get the bartender's number. If my father asks, you haven't seen me."

"You've got it," I answer automatically. I look for Harlin and find him in the corridor holding two glasses of wine while waiting by a nude, white marble female statue—looking like he's really concentrating on it. Especially the top half.

"Double-fisting drinks tonight?" I ask as I approach.

"It's for you. Figured you'd come back empty-handed." He looks back casually and passes me the glass before motioning to the statue. "Do you think her nipples are disproportionately large?"

I step next to him, both of us staring over the naked woman in front of us. "Maybe a little," I say seriously. "But I think it's open to interpretation."

"Most good art is." Harlin lifts his glass for a sip and then turns to me, his eyes a little glassy. I wonder if he had two drinks in his hand before these. "How's Sarah?"

"Bad."

"Anything I can do?"

"Not unless you want to go track down some high school boys to beat up."

He seems to consider it. "Ask me again in an hour."

I look around the room, taking it all in. The art. The people. I'm living and everyone is seeing me. Harlin sees me. I turn to him. "Do you remember that time we went for donuts in Vancouver?" I swallow hard, suddenly scared of what he'll say.

He smiles softly. "You mean when you *dragged* me to get donuts in Vancouver at three in the morning to prove they weren't better than VooDoo's?"

"Yeah. That time."

"Of course. You were wearing my T-shirt and when we got back, Jeremy nearly had a coronary because he thought we'd been out drinking."

"And you told him to relax. It was only decaf." I giggle and suddenly, I feel light. He remembers. Even the smallest detail, he remembers.

I'm not going to become a Forgotten. I'm beating it. I smile and sip from my glass, leaning into Harlin.

He finishes off his wine before reaching over to take my mostly full glass. He downs it and then puts them both on the tray of a passing server before grabbing another one for himself. I narrow my eyes at him. "What?" he says. "You can't handle your alcohol. And besides, they're free."

"Doesn't mean you have to have twenty."

"Sorry, Charlotte," he says loudly enough to get a few stares from the people around us. "It's too noisy. I can't hear a thing you're saying."

"Oh my God, shut up."

"Now," he says, squeezing my fingers playfully, "let's go find more naked things to stare at!"

Harlin reaches in his pocket to peek at his phone, and then slides it back in. I look sideways at him. "Who is it?"

"No one," he says, glancing over the room and avoiding my eyes.

I tsk and reach into his pocket to take out his phone. He doesn't try to stop me and when I check it, I see he has six missed calls. "Harlin?" I ask.

"My mom," he answers, so I don't bother scrolling. "Next weekend would have been my dad's fiftieth birthday and she wants to have a remembrance. I told her I can remember him just fine, but she's going all out." He looks over and his face is pained. "She's having a birthday party and making his favorite dinner. It's sick."

I lower my eyes and put his phone back in his pocket and

in the same movement wrap myself around him in a hug. He's not really hugging me back, but I don't care. I get on my tip-toes toward his ear.

"I'm sorry."

He holds me then, putting his chin on my shoulder. I hate that his mom forces these things on him, but I also hate how Harlin's handling it. It's like he pretends it never happened. If I could use the Need I'm sure it would tell him to deal with his grief. But I can't force the Need to work. It only forces me.

I close my eyes, my fingers tickling the back of his neck. "We should talk about it," I whisper.

"We're at a charity ball," he whispers. "Not really the bare-your-soul type of environment, do you think?" He moves his head so his lips graze my neck. "And all these breasts seem to be staring at me no matter where I am in the room. They're following me."

"Idiot." I laugh, and pull back enough to look at him. I grab his jacket and kiss him, not really able to help myself. We're making out, respectfully (it is a charity event), when someone clears his throat.

Harlin and I turn, still attached at the lips, and see a serious-looking man in a tux standing there. Sarah's father.

"Nice to see you, Charlotte," he says, his voice deep and intimidating. I doubt he means it, and he doesn't even acknowl-edge Harlin.

"Hi." I dart my eyes around for Sarah, but she's nowhere in sight. She might still be at the bar.

"Have you seen my daughter?"

"Daughter?" I'm the worst liar ever. I stare at Sarah's tall, imposing father and try to smile. "She's getting us a table?"

He narrows his gray eyes, and then tightens his mouth. "Is that a question or a statement?"

"Statement?" I'm so blowing this.

He exhales and nods. "Well, then. I guess I'll see you in the banquet room."

Harlin grins as Sarah's father walks away. "You are so subtle, Charlotte. Are you a ninja?"

"Shut up."

"I'm sure he didn't find that at all suspicious."

"Harlin!"

He laughs and kisses the top of my head. "I'll stop," he says. "But where is Sarah? You might want to find her before we sit down for chicken with that man. What will you say if he asks you to pass the mashed potatoes? *Mashed potatoes?*" Harlin finishes, imitating my voice.

I slap his arm and then pull him forward through the ball. He's right. I should find Sarah before Daddy Dearest sends out security looking for her. Just then I see her father standing in the doorway, watching us.

Great. He's probably CIA trained and planning to follow me. I'll lead him right to the bar. "Stop here," I murmur. Harlin and I pause at an abstract—meaning I can't tell what the hell it is—painting.

Harlin is staring at the picture like he gets it, a smug smirk on his face. I study him, not caring about any other piece of art in the room. Just then I feel his phone vibrate in his pocket. His jaw tightens but he makes no move toward it.

"Are you going to answer that?" I ask.

"Do you think the artist knew this work was terrible while he was painting it?"

"No. But I'm not asking about that."

Harlin turns to me, looking serious. "What *are* you asking about, then?" His eyes are narrowed like he's daring me to talk about his mother.

"How you're going to deal with her. You can't just keep ignoring her phone calls."

He smiles like it's a silly statement and turns back to the painting. "Of course I can."

This isn't exactly the moment I was hoping for when I decided to come to this event. I wanted a normal night, a night where Harlin and I would be together, all dressed up and proper. But now I just want him to fix things with his mother. I'm tired of him keeping everything bottled up.

Harlin continues to stare at the painting, sipping from his wine glass. "The brush strokes on this are too wide," he says.

"She's grieving, Harlin. Maybe she needs you to pull her out of it."

Harlin pauses mid-sip, and then lifts the glass to finish it off. When he's done, he sets it on the base of a statue and looks sideways at me. "Let's get out of here."

"What? We haven't even eaten yet."

"Let's leave for California right now and never come back."

I'm completely caught off guard, and step toward him. "I can't just leave," I whisper. "What about Mercy?"

Harlin's mouth curves into a smile and he takes my arm, resting his forehead against mine as he stares into my eyes. "Run away with me," he breathes, smelling sweet from the wine. It's intoxicating. "Run far away with me."

I feel a rush of electricity and my body warms considerably. "Where would we go?"

"Anywhere, as long as I'm with you."

Butterflies flutter in my stomach, and I close my eyes. I can feel how much he needs me, how much I need him.

"You have me forever," he whispers. "I'm yours."

"Mm . . ." I'll run away if he wants. I'll go anywhere as long as I can feel like this—so beautiful and calm. I feel alive.

"Good," he says, leaning forward to kiss me softly. "And you only have to do one thing for me."

"Anything."

"Don't talk about my mother again."

I gasp and pull out of his arms. "Are you serious right now? You just said all that stuff to get me to stop asking about your mother?" My cheeks prickle with embarrassment, a bit of anger.

"No, baby. I meant every word," he tries to explain, touching my hand. "You know I did."

I yank away. "You're an ass," I murmur, and move over to the next painting.

I fold my arms over my chest, ignoring Harlin as he comes

to stand next to me. He presses his shoulder against mine, then leans down, brushing his lips against my ear.

"I'm sorry." He says it so softly it's just a breath. "I love you," he repeats over and over, putting his hand on the curve of my back. I close my eyes and lean into him, letting him put his arm around me.

I want to spend forever with him. I want that to be true. But I have to fight the Need to keep him. To stay alive.

Harlin kisses the top of my head, just as I open my eyes to stare at the painting in front of us.

There are angels in the clouds beating back red and black devils crawling out from underneath the ground. I can't tell which side is winning, and I don't know what it's symbolizing. But I feel like I know more about it than I want to.

CHAPTER 17

According to the bartender, Sarah got a drink and his phone number. But then she left and he didn't see which way she went. Harlin and I had wandered out to the back lawn, but she wasn't there, either. And now it's time for dinner.

"She'll show up," Harlin says as he pulls out my chair for me. I look around nervously and he sits down. I'm not sure I can cover for Sarah at this point. Where the hell is she?

Immediately, I feel Sarah's father's eyes on me from the next table over. But I pretend not to notice him and make a show of saving the seat next to me, telling people loudly that she's in the bathroom. Not super classy, but it's all I can think of on the spot.

I check my phone all through the starter salad and give Harlin my roll because I've lost my appetite. I'm completely worried now. Sarah's been gone for close to an hour.

As the appetizers arrive, I see her father toss his napkin down on the table and walk toward us. Harlin coughs and nudges me with his elbow, and my heart begins to race. I turn innocently to look behind me, and Sarah's dad is standing there.

"Oh, hi, again!" I say. Lame.

"Where is my daughter?" he asks, not bothering with the niceties anymore. He folds his arms over his well-tailored jacket.

"She's not back?" I ask, looking around.

He bends down over me. "Cut the nonsense, Charlotte. Go get her. Now."

His voice demolishes me, making me feel small. I nod quickly and scramble up, nearly knocking over my water glass. I shoot a look at Harlin, who is glaring at her father, almost like he's ready to fight.

"Harlin," I say quietly. When he looks over at me, I shake my head. Harlin curls his lip like it'll kill him to not punch the man, but then he turns and takes a shrimp from my cocktail.

"I'll be right back," I say to both of them and jog through the room, my heels clicking. When I get out into the lobby, I call her phone but she doesn't answer, and I look toward the back door. I can't return to the dinner without her.

The kitchen is buzzing as the servers plate up the entrees

and I make my way through to the loading dock. I have no idea where else to look. I dial her again and then put the phone to my ear as I push out the exit. The minute the heavy metal door closes behind me, I hear the familiar sound of her ringtone—"Just A Girl" by No Doubt.

I don't see her, but I follow the sound. I'm officially freaking out as I start to walk faster, suddenly afraid that she's been hurt or kidnapped.

"Sarah?" I call out, walking around the Dumpster. Just then, I see her heel poking out from the other side. I run to her.

She's lying there on her side, her red hair fanned out around her. There is an empty bottle of tequila near her hand and bunch of foamy puke next to her head. I kneel down and turn her face toward me.

"Sarah," I say again, trying to wake her up. Her eyes flutter, but then she's out again. Checking the bottle, I see that it's empty and I wonder if she stole it from the bar.

She gags and turns her face out of my hand to puke next to me. Not much is coming out and she seems to choke on it. She's barely coherent as she holds herself up, gagging.

"Did you drink this whole bottle?" I ask. She moans something but I can't understand her. I dial Harlin. I have to take care of Sarah—get her out of here before her dad finds her. She needs a doctor.

Harlin laughs quietly when he answers. "Sorry, Charlotte. I'm in the middle of this really fancy dinner. Can I call you back?"

"I need you."

"Where are you?" And I can hear his chair push away from the table and the sound of his breathing quickening as he hurries out of the banquet room. He is my hero.

"Through the kitchen toward the loading dock. Hurry. We need to get Sarah to the clinic."

He hangs up, and I brush back Sarah's hair now that she's done puking. "Did you drink the entire bottle?" I ask again.

She smiles, her face blotchy, her eyes unfocused. "The whole damn thing," she slurs. "Tell my father that."

"You might have alcohol poisoning," I say, even though she's not listening. She's drifting in and out. "You shouldn't have done this," I whisper. "I shouldn't have let you."

Heat burns into my skin and I feel it begin. *No.* I force myself to stay near Sarah, but it's hard. The Need is pulling me back into the party. It's like it doesn't care that Sarah needs my help now. Like my life and my loves don't matter—just some higher purpose.

"Stop," I tell myself. I won't leave Sarah, not when she's here like this. The Need has to wait. But as I resist the pull there is a tearing pain through my chest.

I fall to my knees, scraping them on the concrete. Oh God. Where's Harlin? The metal door at the back of the building bursts open and slams into the bricks. Harlin jumps the stairs and he's running to me, his dress shoes clacking on the pavement.

"Charlotte?" he yells. "What happened?" He takes me by

the arms, helping me up. I collapse into him.

I won't go with the Need. It can't have me. I won't let it! I grit my teeth and swallow down the pain. "Sarah," I say. "She's sick. We have to get her to Monroe."

"Monroe?" he asks. "Charlotte, if something's wrong with her, we should get her father and take her to a hospital. Not the clinic."

"She's drunk, Harlin. He'll freak. Maybe even kick her out of her house." I'm so worried about her and yet the Need is trying to take me away, take me back inside that party.

Harlin looks and sees Sarah curl up on the ground, dry heaving. He lets go of me and darts over to her, kneeling down next to her.

The minute he lets me go, I start wheezing. My body is demanding I go back into the museum, back into the dinner. There's something there I have to see.

Harlin looks at me. "Are you having an attack?"

"I'll be fine. I have an inhaler at the clinic." No I don't, but I'm hoping the farther away from the Need I get, the easier it'll be to fight. I have to do it this time. I have to fight.

"Damn it, Charlotte!" he says. "Why didn't you tell me you were having an attack? Stop keeping things from me!" He scoops Sarah into his arms. Her body hangs limply. "Let's go," Harlin orders without looking at me, making his way around the side of the museum instead of going through the kitchen.

I try to step away, but pain splinters in my head, calling me back. It's like walking against a current. Harlin runs ahead, carrying Sarah to the town car. I try to move faster, but my bones feel like they might pull away from my body, just rip right out of me.

Just as I round the front, it's too much. I fall into the cool, damp grass, but get to my knees and begin crawling. I'm losing focus, getting fuzzy. But I choose Sarah—I choose my life—over the Need.

Harlin's out of my sight, somewhere in the parking lot, and for a second I consider going inside just to stop the pain. It might not take long and the idea of euphoria I get after makes me moan for it.

No. If I do that, if I continue to give in, it'll destroy me. I have to stop it now. There's still time to stop it.

Gripping the grass with my fingers, I pull myself forward. I'm close to the sidewalk now. Just a few more yards. My chest is tightening.

I hear the sound of feet and look up in time to see Harlin running in my direction. He came back for me. There's a small relief to my pain as I feel his strong arms wrap around me, helping me to stand.

"You need to go to the hospital," he murmurs. "Monroe's not helping you. You look terrible."

"Thanks, honey," I choke out. He exhales in exasperation and he leads me toward the waiting car.

"I had to give the driver fifty bucks to not call Daddy Warbucks in there," he says as he opens the door. "So remind Sarah that she owes me." But I can hear in his voice that he's worried. About both of us.

I nod absently as I get in. Sarah is sprawled across the seat and I move her legs to sit next to her. The pain is so strong that tears are streaming down my cheeks.

This is it. I don't know what's going to happen, but I know it hurts like hell. I close my eyes as we pull away, driving toward the clinic. The minute we're off the property there is a pain in my shoulder, like I've just been burned with a hot poker. I wince and glance toward Harlin. He's leaning over the seat, giving the driver directions.

I take the moment to slip the sleeve of my jacket over to find the source of pain. It's on fire. At first I see only gold, more than ever covering the skin. But at the high point of my bone, I see something different and it terrifies me. Because in place of the gold there is a cracked, gray circle. And it looks like death.

CHAPTER 18

I pull my sleeve back over the spot, my eyes wide and burning with tears. What's happening to me? I try to take in a breath, but I can't. Panicked, I look out the window to see the museum—and my Need—get farther and farther away. I gasp again.

The pain is overwhelming, but it's the cracked flesh that's scaring me. I feel my fingertips tingle, like there's no circulation. The museum gets smaller in the distance as the first spots start to come across my vision. My face has gone numb; my lips feel cold. The world tilts.

"Charlotte." Harlin moves to kneel on the carpeted floor of the car. "You're turning blue!" I meet his eyes, not responding, not sure I can. I'm almost ready to welcome the dark when I feel him touch my hand.

And suddenly, a short breath enters my lungs. I just need Harlin. I lean forward and hug him, my face buried in his neck. He's warm and still smells of cologne. I'm only getting air in short bursts, but it doesn't matter. I cling to him.

"Monroe," I whisper.

"No." Harlin shakes his head, but doesn't let me go. "We're going to the hospital."

I can still feel Harlin's hand in my hair when the world around me fades away. Before I can make sense of the change . . .

I'm on the bridge again, rain pelting me. I know I'm supposed to climb on the metal railing but I take a few steps away from it. Suddenly, gold starts to glow around me and I look down to see my skin running off in flesh-colored streams of water. I clasp my hand over my forearm, trying to keep my skin on. But then I realize it's just makeup washing away. And underneath, I'm only gold.

Harlin calls my name. My heart bursts in my chest when I see him running toward me, but I quickly cover my face. I can't let him see me like this. I can't let him see the gold.

I feel a tug and bring my hands down, but Harlin is gone. Instead it's Monroe standing in front of me, yelling. But his words are silent. All I can hear is rain, loud enough to make me wince and want to cover my ears.

But over and over, he mouths, *Jump!*

I push him back and move against the railing, grabbing it tightly. "No!" I look over the side to the dark, rough waters below. I'm terrified of falling.

Now! he silently screams, but I shake my head. And then my heart stops.

Onika appears from behind Monroe. Her face is beautiful again, not cracked and decayed like that one vision. She's not getting wet, even though it's raining. She puts her hand on Monroe's shoulder, but he doesn't react. It's like he doesn't even know she's there.

She smiles at me while in the distance sirens blare as flashing lights enter the on-ramp of the bridge.

Monroe's talking quickly and his eyes are closed as Onika snakes her body around him, whispering in his ear in unison with his mouth moving. It's as if she's telling him what to say.

"Stop!" I scream. It's freaking me out and I'm so scared. I don't know what's real anymore.

With nowhere to go, I climb onto the railing and grip the cables, trying to keep my balance. To get away from them. I glance back over my shoulder and look down again at the choppy water.

Then the scene freezes, the rain suspended in the air, making the world around me distorted. I find Monroe as he stands, now alone, with his eyes closed. I'm about to call to him, but then he slowly looks up at me and whispers, "Jump."

"I think she's coming around."

There's a jolt and I'm awake. I feel disoriented as I glance around at the familiar white walls decorated with posters about STDs. I'm at the clinic.

I close my eyes again. "So I'm not dead?" I ask, my voice barely a whisper. Even though I know where I am now, I can still feel the rain against my skin. The wind swaying me on the bridge. The word "jump" is still in my ears.

"Hardly," Monroe says. I'm startled by how close his voice is and I turn to see him sitting next to me in a chair. His eyes are narrowed as he looks me over. "You gave your boyfriend a good scare, though," he says in a tight voice. "Had to give you a steroid to open up your lungs. Why do you think you had this severe an attack, Charlotte?"

"Stress." I manage to sit up. Harlin is sitting on a stool in the corner, leaning forward with his elbows on his knees and his hands over his mouth. He looks terrified.

"Hey," I call. He doesn't answer, he just stares at me and blinks back tears. "What?" I ask, and suddenly, I'm scared that he saw my skin, that he knows I'm a freak.

He sniffles and rubs roughly at his face. "You passed out," he says quietly. "And I couldn't wake you up. I thought you were dying. I—" He stops and covers his mouth again. Monroe was right—I had scared the crap out of him.

"Come here," I say, and pat the space next to me on the cot.

"Charlotte," Monroe begins, but I look at him sharply. He raises his hands like he gives up and stands, backing away. I have plenty to talk to Monroe about, but Harlin comes first. He always comes first.

Harlin walks over, his eyes red and his beautiful face a

little blotchy. "I don't know what to do anymore," he whispers. "You get worse every day."

And my heart breaks. I fought the Need and it almost killed me, it *is* killing me. The more I slip away, the more I'll hurt Harlin. I don't want to hurt him, but I don't think I can let him go.

I reach out my hand to him and he takes it, before sitting down next to me. He gathers me in his arms, and rests his cheek on the top of my head. I close my eyes, listening to his slow heartbeat. I relax.

Monroe leaves but I can feel him glaring as he does. When I hear the door shut, Harlin exhales. "Monroe is pissing me off," he says quietly.

I prop myself up on my arms and look Harlin in the eyes. "Why?"

"Because he's lying too."

I swallow hard. "What do you mean?"

Harlin scoffs and shakes his head. "You're both lying to me, Charlotte. How stupid do you think I am? I know what asthma is. And I know that you shouldn't be having attacks every day and nearly dying. And when I ask him . . . he's like you. He's hiding something."

His face hardens in anger. And I don't know what I can tell him. I have to keep lying. "It's asthma."

"Shut up." Harlin moves away, turning his back on me. "Don't bother talking if you're not going to tell me the truth."

"Harlin." He's being harsh, and it's making my chest feel

192

raw, hurt. He doesn't answer and I wrap myself around him from behind. I put my face against his warm neck.

"I'm sorry," I whisper. "Don't leave me."

Without a second's hesitation, Harlin turns into me and cups my face with his hands. "I'm not leaving you, Charlotte," he says. "I'm trying to keep you."

His hands are rough on my face. I lean in and press my mouth to his, kissing him softly, the way he usually kisses me. But instead of responding the way I expect, he pushes me back down on the cot and kisses me hard. Desperately.

I suddenly wonder if it means something more. I wonder if he's saying good-bye. But he continues to kiss me with an urgency I haven't felt before. And when we're out of breath, he buries his face in my hair and holds me tight to him.

"Wait," I gasp, looking around the room. "Sarah?"

"She's okay."

"Where is she?" I try to remember the last time I saw her. She was lying on the seat of the town car, unconscious.

Harlin's throat clicks as he swallows. "Monroe called Sarah's father the minute he saw her. He said he couldn't treat her without her dad's consent."

I gasp and pull away. "But he treats me all the time!"

"No offense, Charlotte," Harlin says, "but Mercy doesn't own half the city. Monroe has to cover himself."

"That doesn't mean—"

A booming voice echoes from the waiting room and Harlin and I exchange a glance. Sarah's father is here.

"I have to go out there." I climb off the cot but Harlin catches my arm.

"Maybe you shouldn't. Let's stay out of it."

"No." I pull away from him and start walking to the door when I feel the Need come back, slowing creeping inside my chest. But it's changed somehow. Not as overwhelming, and almost . . . irritating. It puts me on edge.

Harlin follows as I make my way out into the lobby. Sarah's parents are there, still in their formal wear. Her mother's hair is red, but she doesn't have the same spirit as her daughter. Maybe she did once, but now she's not much more than a trophy wife with a Botoxed forehead and plastic boobs.

I pause at the thought, surprised at how cruel I sound. I'd never really disliked her before, but right now, I feel unexplainable hatred. I shake my head, trying to get rid of the feeling, but when we come into view, Sarah's father turns. His dark eyes bore into me as they narrow.

"You," he says, pointing. "What did you do to her?"

"Me?"

"You said she was in the bathroom. Where was she? What did you give her?"

"Why would I give her anything?" I'm confused by his accusation. "I had nothing to do with this!"

A look of disgust crosses his face. "I should have known better than to let her hang around with you. No good—"

But then Harlin is there, standing in front like he's taking a bullet for me.

"I suggest you shut up. Charlotte is your daughter's friend. Her only friend. I think maybe you owe her an apology."

"I will do no such thing!" he yells.

"You're such a prick," Harlin says to him, and then turns away, putting his arm protectively around me.

My mouth twitches with a smile. My boyfriend is so eloquent. For a second, I wonder if Sarah's dad is going to argue, but he doesn't. Instead he storms over to the receptionist.

"I want her released *now*," he says, pounding on the desk. "I'm taking her to a real hospital."

Rhonda sucks at her teeth and types something into the computer as the door to the back opens. Monroe walks out, pushing Sarah in a wheelchair. "Don't bother, Rhonda," he says toward the front desk. "I've already taken care of it."

Sarah looks terrible. Her mascara has run under her eyes and her hair is matted and tangled. Her lips are red and smudged. She glances up to meet my eyes and gives me a little shrug before she's surrounded by her parents.

I listen to Monroe talk to them. He tells them that she has a mild case of alcohol poisoning but that he gave her charcoal to vomit it up. That she needs fluids and rest. Monroe finishes by putting a steady hand on her shoulder and telling them she'll be okay, physically. He doesn't know that her father has driven her to this. And that I didn't stop her from drinking. I wish I had.

Her mother holds Sarah's arm as she stands up, and her dad brushes back her hair. And for a second, I see a different side of them. Like maybe they love her. And to be honest, I'm jealous that she has a family to care about her. I have Mercy and Alex, but what about my *real* family?

Again I shake away the strange thoughts popping in my head. Mercy is my mom and I've never doubted her love. What is going on? I don't feel like myself.

Harlin's hand slips into mine and I'm suddenly comforted. He's always there when I need him. He's my steady heartbeat.

Sarah and her parents pass by, her father staring straight ahead like I'm not worth his time. But Sarah glances over and offers a sad, small smile. She looks humiliated.

"Sarah," I start to say, but suddenly Monroe is in front of me, a stern expression on his face.

"We need to chat," he says.

"No." Harlin wraps his arm around me. "You're done with her. She's had a long night and—"

"Harlin," Monroe says, looking at him patiently. "This is about Charlotte. You can wait out here if you like, but I need to speak to my patient. Now." Then Monroe glares at me like I should agree.

But if I agree now, my boyfriend will be furious with me. He already doesn't trust me. I straighten and look at Monroe.

"I'm sorry, but—" I start to say, just as he reaches into his pocket. He pulls out the black journal, but doesn't mention it. Monroe's right. We do need to talk.

I turn to Harlin. "I have to see him," I whisper. "I promise it won't—"

His face clouds over quickly. "Of course you do, Charlotte.

Don't let me stand in the way of your secrets." Harlin breaks away from me and I'm devastated as I watch him leave. But at the last second he pauses at the glass door. He looks over his shoulder at me, his face drawn. Tired.

"I love you, Charlotte," he says simply. And then he's gone.

As the door closes I wipe at the tears that have spilled over onto my cheeks. I'm ruining everything by lying to him about the Need.

Monroe shifts uncomfortably. "Help me stop this," I hiss. He glances cautiously at Rhonda, who's watching us, before reaching out to grab me by the arm.

"Get in my office. You have a lot of explaining to do."

I sit across from him as he opens his desk and puts the journal in there, locking it. He pulls a small bottle from his pocket and swallows a pill quickly from it. Then he looks up at me, his blue eyes narrowed. "You stole from me."

"I had to. You wouldn't tell me anything."

"I told you what you needed to know."

"Where are the final pages?"

"They're not your concern."

"The hell they're not!"

Monroe exhales hard, and then studies me for a second with a look of disgust. "Take off your shirt," he says.

I'm startled. "No."

He tsks. "Don't be difficult, Charlotte. I want to see what you've done to yourself. Show me your skin."

He knows. Somehow he knows about my dying flesh, and suddenly I don't want to show him. Anger wells up inside me.

"Come on," he says impatiently.

"Go to hell."

"It's there, isn't it?" he asks. "You feel the shadows on your soul, don't you?"

My eyes snap to his and I nod slowly. "It's hate," I say. "I feel hate."

"Let me see." He walks around his desk to stand in front of me, his mouth a thin line of concern.

Slowly I unbutton the navy jacket, biting hard on my lip as I slide it off my shoulder. Monroe gasps. I turn to look where he's staring. My gold—it's nearly gone. The glow is replaced with something horrible. An unthinkable gray, so cracked and dead, like it's sucking the life out of me—splintering the skin as I watch.

"What's happening?" I cry out, truly afraid.

"What have you done?" Monroe stumbles back, knocking into his desk.

"The Need hit at the event, but I didn't go to it. I helped Sarah instead. I thought that if I fought the impulses, this would all go away. That I could beat it like Onika did."

"You're fighting it?" he asks in a hollow voice.

"I don't want to disappear, Monroe. I'm not ready to go." I start to sob. "People are forgetting me sooner. Even Alex and Georgia. Even Mercy. I'm fading. And I'm not ready to go." My voice breaks and I pull my jacket on and wrap my arms around myself.

"I can't watch it again," he says, almost to himself. "I can't."

I sniffle and look up at him. "Watch me dissolve?"

"No," he says, like I'm confused. "Watch you fight to live. You don't understand, Charlotte. You can't stay here."

"But I want to." I sound like a begging child.

"It's not possible. And if you fight . . . it's horrible. It's so horrible."

"Is this what happened to Onika? Did the Need do this to her?" Was Onika dead underneath the beauty that I saw, like in my vision? Was the real her this grotesque?

Monroe squeezes his eyes shut. "No. The Need didn't do this to her. The Shadows did."

I stare at him, goose bumps rising on my arms. "What are you talking about? There was nothing in your journal about Shadows."

My skin begins to itch, like a slow crawl stretching over me. It's the spot. It's growing. "What happened to Onika?" I ask. "I have to know now."

He winces at the sound of her name, then takes in a deep breath. "I loved her so much. And like you, she wanted to fight it. But it ruined her."

"What happened?"

"When she had first started losing her skin, we tried to cover it with makeup. But every day a little more of her was gone. Soon, no one could remember her anymore—except me."

"How did you try to stop it?" Hope wells up in my chest. There could be something, a small detail, a piece of the puzzle that could cure me. If I figure out where he went wrong, I might have a chance.

"I tried a medical approach, combination of pills, toxins even. Anything that I thought could help. And when she started to hold back her compulsions, she told me it was working." He looks at me. "But she was keeping secrets. Terrible secrets."

His words make me think of Harlin and how he knows that I'm keeping something from him. "What sort of secrets?"

"That the Shadows had come for her, trying to tempt her away."

I shake my head. "I don't understand. What is a Shadow?"

"A place devoid of light. A *soul* devoid of light. It will eat your glow and turn you into one of them. Walking Shadows."

I want to rip my nails through my flesh and scrape off the gray.

"You know how you help people, Charlotte? How you save them? The Shadows are the opposite. They drain the light from the universe. They're evil. They spread evil."

"Then why? Why would anyone go into the Shadows?"

"To be remembered. After Onika turned toward the Shadows, people didn't forget her anymore, and she was so beautiful. A showstopper." He glances away as if lost in a memory. "I thought that maybe she'd done the right thing."

"Then what happened?"

"You can't hide from the universe, not in a human form. The body will wear away eventually. Onika found that if she gave into her evil impulses, she could keep her form—make herself stronger. It turned her into a monster, and when I wanted her to stop, she disappeared into the darkness."

"So . . . she wants me to become like her?"

"She needs you to. She wants your light, Charlotte. She has to do terrible things to stay here, and that includes destroying the good. If you let her win, you'll be a Shadow and you'll have to hunt for Forgotten too. You'll have to change them."

"Why would she think I'd go along with that? It's crazy. It's—"

"Onika gave up the light for me, to stay with me. Maybe she thinks you'd do the same for Harlin?" He tilts his head like he's considering the answer to his question.

"I won't. But maybe there's another way to—"

"No," he says loudly. "There is no other way. You must transform, otherwise you'll be bound here, Charlotte. Forever."

My shoulder starts to throb under my hand, and I try to push away the small voice that's telling me that forever-bound sounds a lot better than forever-gone.

"When's the last time you saw Onika?" Monroe asks, turning away from me to go back behind his desk.

"Yesterday, maybe? Or the day before. She comes to me in my visions, mostly, so it's hard to really remember."

"Interesting. I wonder if she appears in visions because they're easier to manipulate than real life."

"I'm not sure."

Monroe sits down on his chair and rests his elbows on the cluttered top of his desk. He looks exhausted. "I'm so sorry it's happening like this," he says. "I've really tried to keep an eye on you all this time. I didn't want the Shadows to find you too soon. And I'd hoped you wouldn't meet anyone—a boy. I didn't want you to have to make a choice."

"Oh, thanks." So Monroe wanted to take away my own will? How is that fair? How is that love?

"It would have been easier," he says. "It wouldn't hurt this much. You're special, sweetheart. You have to believe in that."

"I don't want to be special. And I definitely don't want to be a freaking burst of light. I want to live, Monroe. I want to live here, with Harlin. Like we'd planned." I have to close my eyes as the tears roll out. I miss him so much it's making me ill.

"I can't help you fight it," Monroe whispers to me. "I love you too much to do that. But I can help you fill the Need. Stay in the light."

"You really can't stop it?" I ask. Please. Please.

Monroe's eyes glass over as he stares back at me. "No."

Inside I'm flooded with grief. Absolute, miserable grief. I get up from the chair, my body feeling heavy and slow. "I have to leave," I say.

"I'll remember you," Monroe says. "It's near the end, and from here on out, it's going to be hard. Your family and friends will start to forget."

I offer him a sad little smile. "They already have." Then I walk to the office door, wanting to call Harlin, but remembering that I have to go back to the museum first. I have a Need to fill.

CHAPTER 19

I catch the bus back to the museum. When it drops me off a block away, I feel the Need hit me again full force. Even though it has been pulsating through my bones the entire time, the minute I'm outside it doubles me over. I'm struck with incredible pressure through my chest, my head. I stumble to the bench and sit.

There's no relief. I decide to move, to finish this before it gets worse. Slowly, and still in heels, I limp toward the museum. The charity event ended a while ago, but now there are custodians cleaning up.

The front door is propped open with a trash can and I slip in without them noticing. My heels click on the tile floor of the lobby and I freeze before reaching down to slip them off.

I close my eyes and try to feel where I'm supposed to go. My body is hot—on fire—and it's pulling me back toward the exhibits, back to the banquet room where we had dinner.

I'm pretty sure everyone is gone, but before I can second-guess it, it's like I'm pulled forward and soon I'm walking, hoping that as I get closer the pulsing in my head will stop. I'm a puppet, moving on invisible strings as I pass through the main room and back toward the banquet room.

As I reach the huge double doors, my vision begins to blur. I look around, hoping no one is inside the room, but I can't stop now. I pull open the door and walk in. Out of the corner of my eye I see a man in a light blue uniform.

"Miss," he says, "you can't be in here. We're cleaning."

I don't answer him. I'm being pushed and prodded toward the table, toward where I was sitting.

"Miss!" The man's voice sounds agitated but I'm still walking.

I pause at the table where Harlin and I sat. The room around me is becoming duller by the second; sounds are getting farther away. I think the man mentions something about calling the police.

I reach out and grab on to the back of the chair, squeezing it as I look for a sign. Then on the floor under one of the chairs, something glows. A rush of air blows through me. I bend down to grab it, bring it close to my face and into focus. It's a business card. But the only thing I can read on it is PORT-LAND POLICE BUREAU: CENTRAL PRECINCT.

Then, like being underwater for too long and bursting to the surface, I suck in a great breath with relief. I fall into the table but steady myself. The absence of pain is amazing.

"Do you need an ambulance?" I hear the man ask, and he seems closer. I turn and look at him, surprised by how young he is. His dark skin is dotted with acne and he's wearing a name badge that says Raphael. And he's watching me like I'm crazy.

"No," I say. "I'm sorry. I just forgot something."

He looks me up and down, pausing at my bare feet and then nods his chin at me. "All right. Well, you need to leave. Place is closed."

I thank him and start walking, the business card clutched in one hand, my shoes in the other. I'm so relieved from the Need that I barely notice another worker as he enters the room after me.

"Who you talking to in here, Raphael?" he calls out. I turn around. But Raphael scrunches his nose and grabs a push broom leaning against the wall.

"What? I wasn't talking to no one." And as he begins sweeping, I lower my head and walk out. I'll go to the police station later, and I'll finish this Need. Maybe even fix that gray skin, get my gold back. And soon . . . that's all I'll be. Gold.

"Have to be kidding me," I murmur as I'm forced off the bus by a compulsion. It's barely eight a.m. and I'm on the sidewalk, the business card clutched in my hand, staring straight ahead at the police station. I'm pushed forward and I put the card into my coat pocket as I stumble up the stone steps of the gray building.

I can't believe the Need is taking me here to counsel some criminal. Why not Sarah's father? Maybe I could tell him not to be such a heartless bastard. Or what about Harlin's mother? The Need could help her see that her obsession with her husband's death is driving her son away. I just want to be able to help the people I know—

My sight starts to blur around the edges, focusing in like tunnel vision. Oh great. How am I supposed to get into lockup if I can't even see? I'm about to panic when I notice a woman sitting in the reception area. She's ultra-thin with an expensive black suit, high heels, and a slicked-back bun. Suddenly a wind blows past me and my vision fades, leaving me blind once again.

There's a glow around the woman, a light golden hue. I'm here for her. An intense heat burns across my back. I hate this part. I hate everything about this.

Knowing that I have to get to the woman, I stumble in her direction. When I'm close she looks up.

"You okay?" she asks in a clipped tone.

I want to scream, *No! I'm not okay! I'm dissolving in front of your eyes!* But instead I whisper, "Yeah. Just bad cramps." I grab the hard plastic chair next to her before sitting down on it. I'm trying to hold myself together, but I wonder if my skin is turning gray or gold. What would all the officers here do if it spreads to my face? Would they be scared of me?

"Are you sure you're okay?" the woman asks. I look sideways at her, about to tell her again that I'm fine, but my eyelids flutter and behind them I see visions.

Kendra Rudolph. I see her growing up as an only child, happy. Her mother was an elementary school teacher and her father was a cop. But when Kendra graduated high school, she had a scholarship to Yale. Her parents had struggled to make ends meet her whole life, and even though they'd given her everything she needed, Kendra didn't want a future like theirs, of barely getting by. She never married, never really had time to date. She's ambitious. She's incredibly ambitious.

I see Kendra sitting in a large office, phone in one hand, file in the other. She's a hotshot defense attorney, but that means putting in lots of hours. But she's willing to do it—because she wants to make partner.

She's expensive to hire, but she keeps her clients from going to jail. And in the past twenty years, she's never lost. Not once. She's protected both sinners and saints. But in the end, she doesn't care which they are. As long as they pay her fee.

I open my eyes and see Kendra staring at me, asking if I'm okay. She's never loved anyone in her life—only herself. Only success.

"It's just money," I whisper. Kendra's aura flares up slightly at the mention of the word and I can feel her desire for it. Her obsession.

I fall back into a vision and suddenly I am her, three weeks from now. I'm in my office, phone at my ear. There's an older woman rambling, promising to pay twice my usual fee if I defend her son. I smile, knowing that it means a new Jaguar, or possibly a vacation to Costa Rica.

But the case will be tough. I've read about her son in the paper. He killed a cop, and those cases are notoriously tough to win. I pick up the day's newspaper again, and the man splashed across the front page is Phillip Windmere, a twenty-seven-year-old trust-fund kid turned addict. It says that evidence was just recovered tying him to the murder of a cop two years ago. It says he—

I gasp, pulled back into the reception area with Kendra. "Harlin's dad," I murmur.

"Excuse me?"

Heat prickles my skin, stinging just as the message comes to me. "You'll win," I say. I cover my mouth, horrified at the words. *No! She can't!*

"Win what?"

I try to resist seeing anything more, but it's like a nail is driven through my head. I scream out in pain and put my palms to my temples. I can feel the room of people watching me. But I can't stop the visions—the Need won't let me free this time. And after seeing what happens when I resist, I'm not sure I can go through it again. The pain. The Shadows.

"In three weeks," I say quietly, unable to look up, "you'll get a call about a client. His name is Phillip. You'll be offered a lot of money to defend him." Tears start rolling down my cheeks. I'm betraying Harlin. I don't want to say another stupid word.

I refuse to help the man who killed Harlin's father. How could the Need put me in this situation?

I start to sob, almost unable to continue, but then I hear the message and pause. My eyes widen as I look up at Kendra. "You can't take the case," I murmur. "Even though it's going to upset the partners at the firm."

"What?" The cutting sound of Kendra's voice tells me she'd never upset the partners, not when she's jockeying for a position to join them.

A calm stretches over me and I give into the light, letting it form my words. I'm so tired now, but also relieved. I say what I'm supposed to. "You've helped many people go free, a few deservedly. But this is different. This man, Phillip Windmere, not only murdered a cop, he also killed a woman a few months back." I pause. "Like Madeline."

I know about a case Kendra won fourteen years ago. She had to defend a man who murdered a young woman named Madeline Strait. The man was so clearly guilty, but in the end, Kendra did her job. A mis-served warrant let that monster go free, and before he walked out of the courtroom, he smiled at Kendra and thanked her.

Left in the courtroom with Madeline's weeping parents, Kendra has been consumed with guilt ever since. She wishes she had never taken that case.

"Madeline," she repeats softly, obviously flooded with the same memories.

I nod, watching the light around Kendra glow and darken

with her sadness. I reach out to put my palm around her wrist. "If Phillip Windmere gets off for this murder, he will kill again. In a few months time he'll break into a home for drug money and discover a sleeping family there. Children, Kendra. You can't let that happen. If you defend him, he'll go free. You have to walk away from the case."

"The partners . . ." she answers, but it's robotic, like maybe she knows what she should do.

"It's *right*," I whisper. "You have to do what's right. Even if it means losing the partnership bid. You'll save lives."

Just then the heat becomes intense and I feel my hand burn into her skin. She yanks away, but the colors of my vision are slowly returning. Her eyes are glassy, and I know she's listening.

I bite down on my lip to keep from bursting into tears. The man who killed Harlin's dad will pay. No one else will ever be hurt by him.

"It'll be for Maddy," Kendra murmurs to herself, staring past me. And in my head I can see that tonight she'll go home and rethink things. She'll lose the possibility of her partnership, but she'll go to a new firm. And eventually . . . she'll run it.

I don't even care about the euphoria at this point, in fact, I'm not even sure it's there. I'm just so overcome with gratitude; I slump down in the hard chair, cover my face and cry.

The Need has helped someone I love. This one time, it gave me a chance to help Harlin. And I can feel that Phillip

Windmere will spend the rest of his life in jail.

A few minutes go by, and when I look up, Kendra is gone. She didn't thank me or say good-bye. I know she probably didn't even recognize me as she left. I take a deep breath and stand up, my body still shaking. No one so much as glances at me as I walk out, and for a second, I worry that I'm invisible. But I bump into an old man and he curses at me, reaffirming I'm still here.

When I get out into the cool fall air, I wipe at the tears on my cheeks. I notice my hands, the skin now missing from both of my palms. But it was worth it for Harlin, I tell myself as I go down the front steps, heading to the bus stop. Because now no matter what happens to me, things will be better for Harlin after this.

For once, I consider that it might be okay—my destiny. It might be okay if I go into the light. For so many weeks, I've fought the Need. And now . . . I'm just so very tired.

CHAPTER 20

As I ride the bus toward home, I know that I have to keep what I learned from Harlin. If he knew who killed his dad, he might go after Phillip before the police could. He might do something that could ruin his life. I can't take that chance.

I take my gloves from my coat pocket and slip them on. Then I check my phone and there's nothing. No missed calls, no messages. I send Sarah a text and ask if she's okay. And I suddenly worry that I haven't heard from Harlin. What if he's forgotten me?

The bus jerks, startling me, and then slows at a stop. Out of the corner of my eye, I see something. I turn quickly and my heart stops. Onika is sitting on the bench with her black boots crossed one over the other and her mouth pulled into a beautiful smile. Our eyes lock and she offers a pageant wave. The bus starts moving again, and I put my hand against the glass. I have to talk to her.

"Stop the bus!" I yell, jumping up. The driver looks over her shoulder at me and I hear a few murmurs from disgruntled riders. The bus slows just past the stop. I run down the aisle toward the open doors, my adrenaline pumping. I push the phone into my pocket as I hurry down the stairs.

"Next time I ain't stopping," the driver calls after me.

I pause on the curb as the bus pulls away and stare at Onika sitting calmly on the metal bench. The street is dead and isolated, and I'm immediately struck with nausea and clutch my stomach. Onika shrugs and the pain fades, leaving me warm all over.

"You don't look happy to see me," she says.

"Monroe told me all about you. What you really are. So why are you still following me?" I walk toward her and she holds up her palms innocently.

"You haven't made your choice yet. Not until that weak body of yours finally gives in. Until then, it's still business as usual for me."

"I'm not falling for it."

"No? Why? Because Monroe Swift is such an honorable man? He'd never lie to you." She grins. "Have you noticed the pills he keeps in his coat pocket?"

"What? No."

"Think. The Vicodin. Percocet. Occasionally a muscle

relaxer. Why do you think he's taking so many pills, Charlotte? Seems unprofessional."

And I do remember seeing Monroe pop a pill or two over the years, but I'd never really thought it odd. We were in a clinic and I just . . . didn't think about it.

"He's hurting," Onika mocks with a fake pout. "Being a Seer isn't a walk in the park, dear. Watching the people you care about leave, over and over. He has to self-medicate somehow. My . . . imagine when you're gone—his last Forgotten. I bet it'll be such a relief for him."

"What are you saying?"

"I'm saying that Monroe wants you to go into the light and set him free. He's not getting any younger. And his headaches sure aren't getting any easier. And once you're out of here, he can have his life back. That's pretty strong motivation, don't you think?"

I step back from her, knowing the times I've heard him complain of migraines. Seeing how he'd wince when I asked about the Forgotten. He looked tormented. I narrow my eyes and glare at Onika. "That doesn't mean he'd—"

"Get rid of you? No. Of course, you're right. He'd never be that selfish." Onika glances around the quiet street and then stands up. "I should really get going. I suspect we'll be in touch, love." As she flips her hair over her shoulder, the pain returns to my gut, making me groan.

I stumble over to the bench and sit, waiting for the pain to pass. And when Onika's gone, it does. I push my hair away from my face, but when I look to my side, I see something next to me on the bench. Is that . . . is that Monroe's journal? Onika must have left it for me, but I'm not sure why, and I'm not sure I should touch it. I look around for her again, but I'm alone.

I can't resist anymore. Picking up the leather-bound book, I feel my heart pounding in my chest. It looks the same and I'm confused as I flip through it, but then I stop. The missing pages!

At the end of the book there are crinkled pages tucked in where there used to be nothing but jagged strips of ripped-out paper.

9/9

I met a little girl today, and I knew it was her. First I saw the light shining through her fractured bone on the X-ray, and then there was the incredible pull to protect her. She's the first Forgotten since Onika. I'd thought that maybe my curse was broken, but now I know that it's back. And she's a seven-year-old named Charlotte Cassidy.

I gasp. This is what Monroe had torn out! Pages about me—about me being a curse?

9/24

Mercy Hernandez is taking care of Charlotte and I'm glad for this. It gives me constant access to her, to watch for signs of her crossover. I now wonder if Onika turning to the Shadows kept me

*from my freedom. I can't let the same thing happen to Charlotte.
The whispers in my head have told me that Charlotte's my last,
and that she needs to cross over. I have to make sure she goes into
the light. I can't survive another Forgotten. I can't.*

10/12

*I've felt a presence lately, like I'm being followed. I fear it's
Onika, looking for my Forgotten. I don't think she'll try to find it
in a child, at least not yet. Charlotte came in today with a cut on
her hand, a deep scrape that required a stitch. She says she fell—
again. This is the second time she's come to me with an injury, and
I suspect the compulsions have started. I hope they speed up soon.
I'm not sure how much longer I can hide her. Or how much longer
I can keep going.*

Cold air prickles over my face as my eyes begin to tear. Was
Onika right? Maybe Monroe never cared about me. Maybe
I was just a way to finish *his* destiny. He never wanted me to
have a choice. He just wanted me gone.

I flip through a few more entries, feeling sick from the clinical terms, the unemotional way he describes me. It's like I'm
not a person at all. He's been studying me like a goddamn lab
rat. The next two pages are the same, just writings about my
life. I'm thirteen, fourteen, fifteen. Each entry preceded by my
medical stats. Like a patient—not a friend. Not family. With
only two pages left, I just let the tears stream down my cheeks.

2/15

There is a boy in Charlotte's life. She's never really expressed interest in dating before, so I was surprised when she mentioned him at work today. I'm worried.

If Charlotte doesn't choose the light, I fear I'll be trapped forever. I used to dream of her on the bridge, standing in the rain, ready to cross over. She would fall and then I would be free to walk away, leaving the journals for the next Seer to carry on.

Only now, my visions of Charlotte have stopped, and I wonder if it has to do with her boyfriend. That maybe he's a Shadow, or that maybe . . . she's falling in love with him. Charlotte has to make the right choice. I'm hoping her process will speed up because I'm tired. So tired.

9/12

It's happened! She's changing and I can't believe how beautiful it is. It's been so long since I've seen it, and now that I have, I'm filled with such calm. Amazement. I know now that it's been such a gift to help this higher purpose, even if it's the hardest thing imaginable.

But this time is different. I know what I'm supposed to do and I know that I want my part in destiny to end . . . but I'm not sure I can let Charlotte go. I care for her. I don't want her to experience the heavy loss that's coming.

"Help her to her end." That is the mantra that's running in my head, a thought placed there by something other than myself. And I know I have no choice but to do what I'm told. But when Charlotte goes over that bridge, the last piece of my heart will go with her.

After I read the last page, I let the journal fall from my hands and onto the cement before I cover my face. I fight back the urge to scream as I squeeze my eyes shut. I'm going to disappear. There is no way to stop it, not unless I go with Onika.

The sound of an approaching bus breaks the silence in the air, and I pick up the journal, sliding it into the pocket of my coat.

When the bus stops in front of me, I climb on, half-dazed. Monroe's been studying me. Even though he claims to care now, maybe it's because he's so close to being free of me. Free of the Need. Can't really say I blame him.

I'm about to lay my head against the seat when I see Sarah's high-rise condo on the water. I wonder if she's home. She hasn't texted or called back, and I'm worried as I jump up to get off the bus.

A doorman stands in front of the building—someone I've known for years—and I smile at him as I pass. But he just nods his head politely without any hello, like maybe he doesn't know me.

Don't let it bother you, I tell myself. Instead I cross the lobby to the call boxes and punch in Sarah's number. When there's no answer I try it again, but after a few minutes, I realize she's not home. What if she's in the hospital? I take out my phone, about to call her again, when the double doors at the front of the building open.

"Thank you, Gerald," she says, waving her hand absently as she walks in. I'm completely relieved to see her. She's okay.

"Sarah!" I yell from across the lobby as she heads for the elevator. She glances sideways at me and then stops, smiling softly. "I texted you," I add when I catch up to her. From this close up she looks bad. Her skin is pale and pasty, like someone with the worst hangover in the world.

"My dad took my phone," she says, looking at the ground. "God, I'm so sorry about last night. I really screwed up."

"Why did you do it?" I ask. "Why would you drink so much? You could have died."

"I was desperate. I just wanted it all to go away." She meets my eyes. "The other night at this benefactors' dinner, Seth asked me to go outside. While we were out there, he walked me over to the side of the building and we hooked up. Then—"

"I already know that," I say.

"You heard?"

A frightened tingle runs over my skin. "No, you told me. At my house, remember?"

Her eyes widen. "No. I haven't told a soul."

"Sarah, you came to my room after I didn't show up for lunch. I was home because I got hit by that car and you—"

"You were hit by a car? When did this happen?"

My breath catches in my chest and I step back. "No," I say, putting my hands over my mouth. I can't handle this. I can't

219

handle her forgetting everything.

She reaches out to touch my arm and her fingers feel like ice. "Oh wow," she says, laying her hand flat on my skin. "You're burning up. Maybe you have a fever." She looks like she just realized something. "That's probably why you're confused. Do you want my driver to take you to the clinic?"

I'm not sure what to do, where to go. "No. I can't go to the clinic," I say, and turn away from her. If she's forgotten, does that mean—?

Without waiting to think about it, I run outside and catch the bus to Harlin's apartment. I need him.

"You look pale," Harlin says as we sit on the couch of his apartment. "You should take off your jacket and gloves." He still remembered me when I arrived, which wasn't exactly great because he was far from happy to see me. But I apologized until I was sobbing on his doorstep. He couldn't turn me away at that point.

I look sideways at him, confused at how normal I feel right now. Even though I'm still a bit out of it, my anxiety is amazingly low. It's like a drug, being with Harlin. "Don't you think it's cute?" I ask, holding out the sleeve of my jacket.

He doesn't smile, obviously still angry. "It's cute, Charlotte. But it's hot in here. You should take it off."

I don't want to fight with him. I want us to be playful. Happy. I narrow my eyes and put my hand on his knee. "Is that all I should take off?"

"I can hear you," Jeremy says as he walks into the room, startling me. "Don't make me sit between you on the couch."

I immediately blush. *Now* Harlin laughs. "Did you just get busted trying to be a smartass?" he mocks, putting his arm over my shoulder. "That's what you get. Now come here." He pulls me into him.

I lay my head against Harlin's chest, and feel his heartbeat. It's steady and strong, like him.

"I don't like when you're mad at me," I whisper.

"I'm never *mad* at you, Charlotte," he says. "I just want things to be like they used to." He kisses the top of my head. "I just want more time with you."

I squeeze my eyes shut, because that's the one thing I can't give him.

The house phone rings and Harlin tenses but he doesn't move to get it. Jeremy sighs heavily and walks by, drinking a carton of juice. "I'm not answering it," he says. "I'm tired of making excuses for you, Harlin. Talk to her."

It's then that I remember the lawyer, Kendra. And how she'll make sure that the man who killed their father will pay. It'll fix them, I think. Fix the fractures of their family. I wish I could tell them. But I know it'll do more harm than good right now. I hate keeping this secret.

Harlin says nothing and I start to feel uncomfortable as the phone rings again and again. Finally, just when I think I'm going to lose it, it stops. The room is quiet until Jeremy swears under his breath.

"Don't start," Harlin says, pulling away from me and straightening up.

"I'm not starting anything," Jeremy answers. "But you can't avoid it forever."

"Thanks, Dr. Phil."

In a swift movement Jeremy reaches out and slaps Harlin upside the head. I move over on the sofa, but Harlin is frozen. Silent.

"Watch your mouth," Jeremy snaps. "I'm not Mom. You can't just—"

Harlin jumps up from the couch, shoulder-bumping Jeremy as he walks toward the door. When he gets there, he pauses but doesn't look at me. "Charlotte?"

I glance at Jeremy but he's still staring at the spot next to me where Harlin was sitting. Then he meets my eyes and tilts his head toward Harlin, telling me to go. I stand and murmur good-bye to Jeremy.

Once in the hallway, I touch Harlin's arm and feel his body relax. He turns suddenly and wraps himself around me, burying his head in my hair. I stumble back, but hold him. He's squeezing me tight and I put my fingers on the back of his neck, whispering in his ear that I love him.

After a minute I take my arms from around him and rest them against his chest. His hazel eyes are sad, tired, and I'd do anything to make it better. But I can't tell him what I know. I can't even promise to stay with him now that the Need is almost done with me.

I get on my tiptoes and kiss him. He lets me, not making any moves as I first kiss his top lip, and then his bottom one. When I pause and look at him, he still doesn't reach for me. "Stop being mad," I whisper before trying to kiss him again.

He doesn't let me and instead holds me back by my arms. He lowers his head so it's even with mine and looks deeply into my eyes. "Tell me what's going on with you." His face is serious, but his eyes are pleading. "Please."

What can I say? What can I possibly tell him that will make sense? "I love you," I say. "That's all there is, Harlin. I just love you."

His mouth opens in surprise, or maybe he's thinking of arguing, but before he can respond, it happens. I'm struck with a shooting heat over my body and I'm doubled over before I can stop it. Harlin drops to his knees, holding me to him.

I've got to pull myself together, get to the Need, but it's so painful this time that I'm not sure I can. Harlin's voice is starting to echo and I know that if I don't move soon, he'll call an ambulance. And I can't go to the hospital.

It's hard, but I straighten, feeling like daggers are in my gut. I pull away from Harlin and lean on the cracked plaster of his hallway wall.

"What's happening?" he says, sounding frantic.

"Cramps," I answer, unable to fully look at him.

"You're lying, Charlotte!" he yells. Suddenly he grabs me by the elbow and spins me around. I'm so alarmed that I temporarily forget the Need. All I can see is how upset I'm making him. "My God," he says, tears falling from his eyes. "Are you dying or something? Is that why you won't tell me?"

"No," I say quickly. But that's not true. Because really, I *am* dying. And I'm about to let him down the same way his father let him down. I'm going to leave him too early. I'm going to leave him heartbroken. I pull my elbow out of his grip and stand close to him, ignoring the pull that's yanking me toward the exit.

"You're lying," he whispers, like he's given up. His face is drained of color as he watches me. Harlin raises his hand and puts his palm on my cheek. I turn into it, but don't take my eyes from his. "I can't do it anymore," he says. For a second his face breaks with the start of a cry, but he shakes his head quickly instead. "I can't be with you anymore."

"What?" I push his hand away. He can't mean that.

"You keep lying to me," he says. "Over and over you lie, sneak around. That's not a relationship, Charlotte. You're killing me."

Before I can argue, he leans forward and kisses the top of my forehead, pausing long enough to make it seem final. And inside, the Need can't compete with the loss I feel. I'm losing everything.

"Don't do this," I murmur as he backs away from me toward his apartment door.

"Good-bye, baby," he says in a hushed voice. He pauses and I wait for him to tell me that he didn't mean it. That this isn't happening. Harlin stares at the floor for a long moment, and then goes inside.

I stand there, my body aching, but my heart feeling worse. Harlin and I had plans. We had a future. I want to bang on his door, explain everything and make him understand. I'm not sure I can go on without him.

But suddenly a thought occurs to me. Maybe this is better, leaving him like this instead of slowly dissolving away. I close my eyes and start to cry. There is a hot burning up and down my arm as if I'm on fire. I push up my sleeve.

The skin falls away as the fabric rubs against it, leaving my entire arm a brilliant, glowing gold. There's no way to hide this now. There's no way.

I start for the stairs, wanting to get out of the hall before someone discovers me. I'll follow the Need and Harlin will forget me. They all will.

It's almost over.

CHAPTER 21

I burst through the doors of Harlin's apartment building
onto the sidewalk and feel the familiar whoosh of air. I stop
and wipe the tears from my face. Right now I just have to get
through this, so that I can go home. I just want to curl up
under my covers and block it all out. Pretend everything's okay.

But being okay is hard to do when the Need is ripping through
my gut. I glance around the busy street and pause. There.

I stumble toward a white van parked at the curb. The side
reads ST. LUKE'S HOSPICE. A woman walks around from the
driver's side and swings open the back doors. I stop, waiting to
see what it is that I'm supposed to do.

She pulls out a black duffel bag before closing the door
(although it doesn't shut completely) and steps over the curb.

She smiles politely at me as she passes and I turn to watch her walk into the apartment building next to Harlin's.

When she's gone, I look back at the van. I'm supposed to open it, see something. I'm so tired now, physically, mentally, and emotionally. I feel like a shell, almost like my own will is gone. At least that's how I feel in this moment.

I walk off the curb and stop in front of the back doors of the van. I wonder if after this, if when this is done, I'll be over.

Resigning myself to this horror, I glance around the back of the van. There are boxes and paperwork everywhere. I search for something to stand out, and soon my vision begins to blur. I reach out my hand like I'm blind and start feeling things, waiting for what will come into focus.

I'm not sure how long I'm there until I brush my fingers over a clipboard and suddenly my chest constricts, squeezing me tight. I look down and focus on one spot.

Warren Bradley—1850 W. Mission Blvd. Apt 715

And then I'm released. I stumble back, my vision clearing but my head spinning. I look up to check if the worker is coming back. I don't see her and I quickly shut the door with a click before jogging down the street.

I start to wonder who Warren Bradley is, but then I decide I don't care. My heart is aching. I've just lost Harlin.

I don't mind walking the twenty or so blocks to the apartment. It may be the last walk I take. The wind is getting colder, whipping over my face but I like the feeling. It contrasts with the sickness in my gut, the one that's making me do this. The

227

Need that has ruined everything.

I get to the building and look up to the seventh floor. The intricate brickwork outside culminates into a large archway, leading to a set of glass double doors. There's a bronze plaque fastened at the entry, telling me it was built in 1890. I wince as a stabbing pain makes its way from my head down to my toes, but I don't double over from it. I almost welcome it at this point. It means I'm almost done.

I walk into the lobby and notice the round tile swirling into a pattern beneath my feet. The walls are rich in mahogany wainscoting at least shoulder-height. I find the elevator and am grateful that there's no one riding up with me. I don't think I can stand still in an elevator and pretend I'm normal. I'm not normal. I've never been.

It seems like forever, but when I get to the seventh floor, the wind blows past me and I smile. I've made it.

I walk down the carpeted hall. Landscape paintings in gilded frames hang on the walls; heavy wood doors block out all sounds of life from within the apartments. With each step I feel myself slipping further and further away.

When I'm in front of Warren Bradley's apartment, I stop. He's waiting for me.

I knock tentatively. There's a rustling from inside, but no answer. I knock again, taking short breaths because it's all I can get in my lungs.

Still no answer. Now I'm beginning to panic because I want in. I want to be done. I'm so tired.

Reaching forward, I turn the door handle and it opens with a click. Under normal circumstances, breaking and entering would seem a bit much, but right now, the Need is so overwhelming, I push open the door.

The room is dark and it takes a minute for my eyes to adjust. There are windows in the living room that I can see from here, but they have shades pulled down, blocking out the light. It smells like antiseptic.

There's a cough from the living room. "You're early. My meds aren't due for another hour," a man says in a raspy voice.

There's a jolt and I'm pushed down the hallway toward him. I'm suddenly scared, scared of who Warren is, scared of what I'll be after this. My mouth is opening, trying to let words escape but they're caught in my throat.

Warren Bradley is lying in the dark in a hospital bed. There is no light in here. I hear him suck in a breath and it's loud, labored. Monroe has told me many times about that sound. The death rattle.

I swallow hard and walk toward him. Even though Warren is not glowing, he has a dull glaze of yellow aura when I get close enough. Next to his bed is a lamp, and I turn it on.

He's staring at me. His lips are dry and cracked, yet he smiles. "You could have skipped me today," he says. Warren wears his graying hair in a buzz cut, and he's tucked up to his neck under a white sheet. I think that once he must have been really handsome. But now . . . now he's skinny and frail.

"I don't have any medicine," I say. My heart is beating hard against my chest and I see his glow flicker, but it's not coming to me. The Need isn't coming out.

Warren furrows his brow. "You're not with hospice, are you?" A look crosses his face, a mixture of fear and relief. "Do you think you could open the blinds?" he asks quietly. "I'd love to see the sunlight again."

His request surprises me and I walk over to raise the shades. The room fills with light and I see how nice it is. Lots of antiques, a brightly woven rug in the middle, and shelves and shelves of books. When I look back at Warren, he's watching me.

"You're not what I expected," he says.

His words freeze me. "What?"

Warren starts to shift in the bed, pulling himself slowly into a sitting position. When he's settled, he waves me over. "Do you think you can sit with me for a while?"

I nod and drag a chair to his bedside. We watch each other until my Need seems to perk up again, pulsing though me stronger every second.

"You're sick," I say, in my own weak voice.

He smiles sadly. "I am."

"What is it?"

"This time? Pneumonia."

I close my eyes and try to see him, see his story, but nothing comes. I begin to wonder if I'm in the wrong place when he holds out his hand to me.

Does he know me? I feel like I'm missing something, but without hesitation, I reach for him. The minute we touch, the world goes black.

I am a boy, my parents are driving the station wagon and we're going to Disney World. I'm so happy. My brother is next to me, talking about his girlfriend, but I just gaze out the window. The scene changes and I'm in high school. I have a lot of friends, but no dates. People don't understand.

Sadness overwhelms me. I'm sitting at my father's bedside and he is an old man now. I'm crying but he keeps his face turned away from me. He won't speak to me. Even now, he won't speak to me.

And then I find Roderick. He's the most loving man I've ever met, and he takes care of me. We take care of each other. We're thinking of adopting, but then I'm at the hospital . . . with Roderick. He's been diagnosed, but no one can know yet. Only me. We'll deal with it together.

"What's your name?"

Warren speaks and it breaks my vision. I sway in the chair and stare at his dull glow, the only thing I can see. I wait for the words to come, and after a second I can speak. "Charlotte."

He smiles. "I've been waiting for you," he says.

Tingles race over my skin. "You have?"

He nods. "Saw you once, when Roderick died. You were in the hospital with him. Of course, not as you are now, but I recognize you still."

My lips part and I want to pull my hand out of his, oddly afraid of his words. But as I meet his eyes, his glow goes out and my vision returns. I see his chest rising and falling slower.

231

He's almost gone and I still don't know why I'm here.

"Your mother?" I ask. "Do you want me to call her?"

He closes his eyes and then shakes his head. "No, she passed away a few months ago. She talked to me though. Apologized."

I exhale, feeling relieved. I thought that maybe I was here to help him reconcile with his family, to heal some of that hurt. But it seems that already happened.

"Then why am I here, Warren?" I don't even mean to ask it out loud. But he looks at me so sadly that I feel my entire body shudder from the sorrow.

"Because I don't want to die alone."

Tears begin to stream from my eyes, hot on my cheeks. I put my other hand on Warren's and squeeze it tight. I am filled with love for him, love that's beyond me. He sniffles and tilts his head to the side. Suddenly his eyes get wide and I straighten, afraid he's passing away. But instead he reaches out with his free hand to touch my cheek, rubbing his thumb across it.

His expression changes to reverence. Amazement.

"It's beautiful," he says, staring at me. "It's so beautiful."

I'm gasping, both horrified and overcome with my own emotions. The Need fades, leaving me weak, but I hold on to Warren's arm. He starts to cry, then laughs, almost rejoicing at the sight of me.

I don't know what to do, so I just stay with him. I stay there until he gets quiet and his breathing slows. And then it stops— his eyes still locked on mine. I wait, hoping he'll take in another breath, but when he doesn't, I drop my head. And weep.

CHAPTER 22

I close the door to apartment 715 with a quiet click and pause in the hallway. Hospice will be here within minutes, so I don't call the cops. But it was hard to leave. I've never seen someone die before, but I'm glad I was here. I'm glad Warren wasn't alone. Before I left, I went to his closet and borrowed a hoodie. I flipped up the hood of the red sweatshirt to hide my face. I tried not to look in the mirror, but eventually I couldn't help it. And the scene wasn't good.

My skin is gone, rubbed away. My face is golden, like my back and my arm. Like my shoulder. I no longer look human. I'm not sure what I look like.

I make my way out to the lobby just as the front door opens with the same woman from earlier, a black bag in her hand.

Careful to not be noticed, I turn toward the mailboxes and take out my phone pretending to talk. I wait until she's in the elevator and gone before I leave. When I get outside I realize that I can't just walk around like this. My face is gold. I don't have a face.

There is only one person I can tell. I text Monroe: *I need help. No skin. 1850 W Mission.*

Within seconds I get a response. *On my way. Stay out of sight.*

I step back to lean against the brick wall of the building and put my hands over my face. I don't know what to do now. I have nowhere to go. Minutes later an ambulance arrives and I move out of the EMTs' line of vision. I'm hidden in the shadows of the alley when they roll Warren out on a gurney, a sheet over his head. I hate that they've covered him like that. He said he wanted to see the sunshine. It takes a considerable effort for me not to run over and yank the sheet from his body. Of all my Needs, he's the only one who saw me. The me underneath.

There's a quick beep of a horn and I glance up to see Monroe's car idling at the curb. For a second, I'm even happy to see him, even though the last time we talked I think I told him off. I walk up to the car and yank open the passenger door before climbing in. Once inside, I turn to him, my head down.

"Let me see," he says.

I'm not sure I want him to anymore. I feel like a freak. But I slowly raise my chin and his mouth falls open before it pulls it into a smile.

"My God, Charlotte," he says. "It's beautiful."

I look away quickly and pull the hood around my face. "I wish you would stop saying that. It wouldn't seem so beautiful if it was your face."

Monroe pulls his car out into the street but doesn't respond. We drive quietly until I look sideways at him.

"I spoke to Onika," I say simply.

Monroe's knuckles turn white from his grip on the steering wheel. His mouth opens like he's going to talk, but he closes it again. He's silent.

"Don't you want to know what she said?" I ask, irritated that he didn't ask. It was kind of a big deal.

Monroe clenches his teeth. "I'm sure it was a bunch of lies, whatever it was."

"She said you were just trying to get rid of me so that you could live your life. Is it true? Am I your last Forgotten?"

"She's trying to get you away from the last person who cares about you, Charlotte. She's trying to turn you against me."

I nearly punch him. "*Care* about me? You've been studying me like a science experiment with that stupid journal of yours." I pull out the book and toss it at him. "You kept me close so that you could watch me. All so that you can be free of your curse. You never would have helped me. You'd have pushed me off the damn bridge if you could have."

He turns to me abruptly. "Yes. You are my last Forgotten, but it doesn't mean this is easy for me. You have no idea what I'm going through."

"What *you're* going through?" I laugh. "What about what

I'm going through? What about everything *I've* lost?"

Monroe stares out the windshield, his eyes blinking quickly as if holding back tears. "I know what you're losing, Charlotte. But you have to listen to me. Don't believe anything that beast tells you. She's trying to tempt you away. She's trying to destroy you."

"You afraid I'm going bad, Monroe? All rotten flesh and evil impulses?"

"I'm not kidding!"

"Do you think I am?" I snap, pulling back my hood. "Look at me! Look what's happening to me!" And all at once the world crashes down on me in a heavy wave. I've lost everything. Lost Harlin. Lost my face. And soon, I'll lose my life.

I'm shaking with sobs as I curl up in the passenger seat. Monroe gently touches my hair. When he speaks, his voice is soft.

"I'm sorry I didn't do more for you," he says. "I wish I could have prepared you better, prepared you for the loss. But I thought trying to keep you hidden was right. I thought it'd keep the Shadows away long enough for you to cross over."

There's a lump in my throat and I swallow it down. "Nothing could have prepared me for this," I murmur into the fabric of the seat.

"It was never just about the Forgotten," he says. "You know I'm going to miss you madly, don't you? You're the only person who tells me off on a daily basis."

I sit up, looking at him. He's crying, his eyes darting between me and the road. Despite our fighting, Monroe means a lot to me. He's like family. He *is* family.

"You're all I have," he says with a quiet whisper. "And despite what you may think, I'm proud of you for being so brave, for doing these things when they're so hard. But I always knew you were a good girl. That's why it's you. That's why the light is in you."

I close my eyes, tears streaming down, and let his words comfort me. "What will happen when I jump?"

"The light will burst out. People will feel a second of love, peace. Everyone will be touched. You will give them a reason to go on."

"And after me?" I ask.

"There will be another Forgotten. And another. Until all the Shadows are gone." He looks over at me.

I nod, wiping at my nose with the back of my glove. "You'll make a sucky father someday," I tell him. "I feel sorry for the kid that doesn't get to burst into light to get out of your house."

He chokes out a laugh. "Is it my sarcasm?"

"No, but I'm guessing you'll expect a complete angel." I grin.

"I suppose I would."

"Plus your accent is totally obnoxious."

"I'll try to remedy that."

I pause, my smile fading as we watch each other silently. "I'll miss you too," I murmur. And then Monroe nods and turns back to the road.

"I have some things at the office," he says. "Some ways to

disguise the transformation—latex and makeup. But it's not completely foolproof. Harlin and Mercy might be able to tell the difference if—" He stops.

"If they can even remember me?"

He nods.

"A rubber face," I say to myself. "Can't I just burst now or whatever it is that I'm supposed to do?" I might as well since I'll never see Harlin again. The thought hurts like a punch, so I push it away. I won't think about him again. I can't.

Monroe shakes his head. "It's not your time yet," he says.

"Do you have the itinerary? I seem to have lost mine."

"Don't be a smartass."

"It's what I do, Monroe."

We pull into the clinic parking area and I wait as he comes around the car to let me out. "Just keep your head down," he says. He adjusts my hood and pulls it down to shield my face as much as possible. He puts his arm over my shoulder, turning me toward him as we walk to the front door. It opens with a jingle. He's moving fast and I nearly stumble.

"Dr. Swift," Rhonda calls, standing up from behind her desk. "You had several calls while you were gone. I told them—"

"Not now, Rhonda," he answers quickly, ushering me forward and to his office. "I have to work with Charlotte on something."

"Who?"

Monroe and I both stop, but I don't look up. My heart is frozen.

238

"Charlotte Cassidy?" he says slowly.

"Oh . . ." I hear in her voice that after working together and knowing me for close to ten years, my name is only vaguely familiar to her. I silently say good-bye to Rhonda.

Monroe shifts on his feet, obviously distraught, and tightens his arm around me. "I don't want to be disturbed," he adds.

"Stop squirming."

"It's cold," I say, cringing every time he wipes the brush along my face. Monroe has created a smooth, latex-based makeup that will cover the gold. But it's thick. It makes me look like I'm wearing too much foundation, but it's better than walking around gold and glowing.

"There," he says, stepping back to admire his work. "Of course, this only really works for the face. It's too complicated to make a batch large enough for the entire body."

I shrug. "No one sees my body anymore." I wonder if, like Rhonda, Harlin has forgotten me already.

"It's for the best," Monroe whispers. I'd told him about the fight with Harlin and how he broke up with me when I wouldn't tell him the truth. I also explained about the lawyer and how the man who killed Harlin's father would go to jail. Monroe agreed that I shouldn't interfere with the Need. That if Harlin knew, he might somehow affect it, and who knows what could happen. He said I did the right thing by leaving Harlin's. I want to believe him.

I hang my head as I wait for the makeup to dry, forcing

myself not to cry so it won't be ruined. "What do I do now?" I ask. I look down at my hands in my lap and pull off my gloves. The glow is bright underneath. I realize that I'm resigned to it. It's just what I am now.

Monroe watches me with a sad expression. "Remember," he says quietly, "you're still you, Charlotte."

I lift my eyes to meet his. "Charlotte doesn't exist," I say. "No one will ever remember me." And the statement in my ears is the most horrible thing I've ever heard. Because I never existed. There is no such thing as me.

"You've helped a lot of people," he says. "They may not remember it was you. But you've changed their lives. Even the ones who weren't your Needs. Mercy, Sarah, Harlin—they'll all remember the love you gave them. That can't be taken away."

"Am I an angel?" I ask, sniffling hard to try to keep away the tears.

"You're more than that." Monroe puts his hand on my shoulder. "And I can promise you one thing: I will never forget you, Charlotte Cassidy."

At least there's that. At least there's Monroe.

The phone on his desk buzzes and we both jump. "Dr. Swift?" Rhonda's voice comes over the intercom. "I'm sorry to interrupt, but we have an emergency."

He looks back at me, and I try to smile. "Go," I say. "I'll call you if I burst into light or something."

He looks at me thoughtfully. "I'll talk to you soon," he

assures me, and squeezes my shoulder before leaving his office.

"Wait, Monroe?" I call as he gets to his door.

"Yes?"

"Do you think I still have time to say good-bye to Sarah?"

He seems to think about it for second, and then meets my eyes. "Hurry."

Monroe walks out and my heart begins to race. *Hurry.* Hurry as in five minutes from now or five hours? I have to see her. I have to say good-bye, even if she doesn't know what the hell I'm talking about.

I stand quickly and check my reflection in the mirror Monroe had left out on his desk. I don't look great, but I don't look awful, either. I figure I can bluff my way through it, blame it on a bad mall makeover or something.

Just in case, I take out my phone and smile when I see that I have a text message that was sent a few hours ago. It's from Sarah.

Frankie's for lunch?

It's a little late for lunch, but maybe I can catch Sarah before she leaves. I shove the phone back into my pocket and rush out, hoping to have one last time with my best friend. Hoping to have one last chance to feel human.

CHAPTER 23

As the bus pulls up in front of Frankie's, I see Sarah walking away with a white takeout bag. I'm so relieved as I run to her, calling out and waving wildly to get her attention.

Sarah glances over and smiles, then nods at me. "Hi," she says cautiously.

She looks better than she did yesterday. Her hair is smooth and her eyes have been made up, but her jacket is long and conservative. It looks like something her father would approve of.

"Sorry I missed your text," I say. "I've had a crazy morning."

"It's okay."

"Have you talked to Harlin at all?" I can't help but hope that he was worried when I left him. Maybe checked in with Sarah.

"The motorcycle guy?" she asks.

I pause. "Yeah."

She smiles a little. "I always wondered what happened to him after he dropped out of St. Vincent's. He was nice to look at." She wiggles her eyebrows like I should agree. "Are you dating him?"

Devastation washes over me. Her expressions are so unfamiliar to me, so . . . cold. I almost can't bring myself to ask.

"Sarah, you know who I am, right?" I ask in a small voice.

A look of guilt crosses her face. "Of course. We were in the same class, right?" She stops, darting her eyes around the sidewalk as a few people pass us. "I'm not going to St. Vincent's anymore. My father thought a private tutor was my best chance to get into an Ivy League school next year."

My heart sinks. I know damn well that Sarah doesn't give a crap about Ivy League colleges. This is something she would tell a person she met at a charity ball. Something she would tell a stranger.

"I'm Charlotte," I say, feeling my life drain out of me. "I'm your best friend."

She steps back and laughs softly, probably trying to discern if I'm joking.

"Best friends? I think I'd remember that, Charlotte."

"We've been friends since Ms. Cavanaugh's seventh-grade gym class," I say. "You forgot your swimsuit one day and were crying because you didn't want to sit in detention alone, so I pretended to have lost mine so that I could keep you company."

Her eyes widen. "How did you know about Ms. Cavanaugh's class?" Her face is pale and I know that I'm scaring her, but I can't stop. I want to remind her of how much I love her.

"And then we went to the junior prom in your dad's BMW while everyone else took limos because you wanted to stand out. Matthew Bower was your date, but you didn't like him because he was a wet kisser." I laugh at the memory, remembering how often she recreated the disaster for me on the back of her hand or on her mirror.

"You're starting to freak me out," she says, moving away from me.

"And I was there at the museum when you drank a bottle of tequila to forget that you never feel good enough for your father. I was so scared for you. Harlin and I took you to the clinic and I needed to know you were okay."

"Are you the one that dropped me off at the filthy free clinic? Are you a stalker or something?"

"No. I'm your only real friend."

"Look," she snaps, lowering her voice to a harsh whisper so as not to attract attention. "I don't know you, and I don't know what your deal is." She looks like she's about to cry and I'm not sure if it's the fact that she's scared or embarrassed that I know about the alcohol poisoning. But it's not for the same reason I want to cry. I miss her. She's standing right in front of me, and I'm missing her already. "Now I suggest you get out of here before I call the police," she finishes, shooting a glance over my shoulder. I turn and see her driver get out and open the back door of the car.

There's nothing I can do. There's not one single word I can say that will make her remember me. So instead, I smile at her, wishing I could hug her one last time, but I don't. I slowly back down the sidewalk.

"Take care of yourself, Sarah," I say. She stares after me. "You're better and stronger than your dad thinks. I've always known that."

Her face crumbles a little at the statement, but she turns and hurries into the waiting town car. I watch as she drives away, out of my life.

When she's gone, I walk slowly over to the bus stop bench and put my face in my hands. My fake face.

On the ride home, I stare out the window, wondering if I'll see Onika this time. I don't. But I know she's not gone. She said she'd see me soon.

I replay images in my mind—mostly of Harlin and me. I ache for him. But I'm not me anymore, not on the outside. Even if by some small chance he does remember me, I can't let him see me like this. I've lost him.

The bus stops at the corner before my apartment building. As I walk off I glance around to see if anyone is staring at me, noticing something's wrong. But like every other day, they say nothing, notice nothing, and I'm glad that I'm not standing out.

I'm relieved when I finally get into my apartment. The smells are familiar and I nearly collapse on the sofa when I walk in. Even though Sarah forgot me, I know that Mercy hasn't, not this soon. I call out her name, but no one answers. I decide that tonight I'll share one last meal with my family and tell them I love them. Even if they won't remember come morning.

I'm still on the couch when Mercy and Alex get home. They're carrying grocery bags and laughing, but when they open the door, they stop and look at me.

"Do you need a hand?" I ask, jumping up.

Alex raises an eyebrow and looks between Mercy and me. "Um . . . hello, breaking and entering. Can I help you?"

My body goes cold. My heart stops. "What?" I ask.

Mercy snaps with her free hand. "Oh!" she says. "Did the agency send you? Are you my new girl? I'm sorry, honey. You just caught us off guard."

I can't answer as I stare back at my family. Alex is sizing me up, the way he does everybody, deciding if I'm cool or not. And Mercy is giving me the same warm smile she reserves for kids she thinks are unloved. But she loves me. She just doesn't remember that.

"What's your name?" she asks kindly.

"Charlotte," I say, tears brimming my eyes.

"That's a beautiful name. It's my grandmother's name," she adds.

"I know."

She tilts her head, wondering how I knew that, I suppose.

Then she shoos Alex in the doorway before closing the door and walking toward the kitchen. She sets her bag down and then comes into the living room where I'm still standing, dumbfounded.

I really didn't think she'd forget. I really didn't believe it. "Where's Georgia?" I ask, wanting to see her one last time too. Wanting to finish all of this.

"You know Georgia?" Mercy smiles.

"Figures," Alex says from the kitchen.

"Oh, shut up," Mercy tells him quickly. "Georgia is leaving us. She's been placed back with her mother. Is that how you found us? Through her?"

I shake my head. *No, Mercy. I never really got to know Georgia, not the way I should have. And I guarantee she doesn't know me.*

"Huh. Okay then, let me show you to your room so that you can get settled," Mercy says and puts her hand on my shoulder. I can't even speak as I follow behind her down the hall. When we stop in front of my doorway she turns to me. "You've already put your stuff in here," she says, surprised. "Well, I'm glad. This is your home now, Charlotte."

I'm surprised to see that my belongings are still here and I wonder what happens when I'm gone. I take another look around and notice one thing missing. All of my photos.

The pictures of Sarah and me that were taped to the vanity mirror are gone, although a faint outline of them still remains. The prom picture on my side table of Harlin and me is now just an empty frame. I miss him, miss everyone so much, but Mercy walks over and pulls me tight to her.

"Oh, honey," she whispers in her thick accent. "You must have been through *something*."

I'm pressed against her white uniform and the smell of detergent that I know so well, but she doesn't know me. She doesn't know me at all. I cling to her, my last touch of my mother. When I pull back I look at her.

"Thank you," I say. "Thank you for everything, Ma."

She smiles. "You're sweet. And honey, I haven't even started taking care of you yet."

I nod, and then motion to the bed. "I think I'm going to lie down for a little bit, if that's okay?"

"'Course," she whispers supportively. "Your first night in a new place is always the scariest."

If only she could remember that this isn't my first night with her. Or my second. I've been with her since I was six. She is my only mother. I run to my bed and lie down and the minute I hear Mercy close the bedroom door, I sob. Cry harder than I ever have in my life. Because I just became an orphan. Again.

CHAPTER 24

It's dark when a stabbing sensation tears through me. I groan and fold over in bed, clutching and shaking. Oh God. It hurts!

I try to focus through the pain, but it's hard. It creeps through my gut and settles in my chest. It's as if someone is sitting on me, restricting my breathing. It's like my body is imploding on itself. It's the worst pain I've ever felt.

Get up, I tell myself. Slowly I drag my legs over the side of my bed, touching at the floor. "I can do this," I murmur. I'm being pulled somewhere, and wherever it is, I'll go gladly. This is unlike any pain the Need has ever given me. My school shoes are in front of my closet and I slip my feet into them, then absently grab the green jacket Sarah bought for me.

Then the pain suddenly disappears. I'm left with a tingling, an almost pleasant feeling. What's going on? I look around the room, unsure of what to do, when I see my phone vibrating on my side table. Cautiously, I move over and glance down. I don't recognize the number.

"Hello?" I ask, looking at the clock. It's three thirty-three.

"Hi, Charlotte," the female voice says. It's soft, the smallest hint of a Russian accent. "Feels better, right?" When I don't answer, she laughs.

"I'll see you at the bridge in twenty minutes," she continues. "I'll be waiting. See you soon, darling."

She hangs up and the minute she does, the pain comes back with a force, knocking me off my feet, ravaging my body. I clutch the sheets of my bed, falling to my knees. I lift the bottom of my shirt to look at my stomach and the sight terrifies me. In the gold there is a small half-moon slit, about the size of a fingernail. It seems to go all the way inside me and from it emanates a glowing white light.

"No," I whisper. "I'm not ready." And then just like that, the pain eases enough for me to stand. I wrap my jacket tightly around myself and grab my phone. This is the end, and Onika is waiting for me. I'll have to face her, even if I'm terrified.

The Rose City Bridge is only fifteen minutes away from my apartment building, and with the streets empty, it doesn't take long for the bus to get there.

I'm sure that my makeup has rubbed off, because people are staring at me. They're turned around in their seats, watching me in frozen amazement. They don't speak at all. When we reach my stop and I walk past them, a couple murmur prayers.

As the bus pulls away, I look at the windows and see that everyone has gone back to what they were doing before. As if they've forgotten me already.

There is a thumping in my head, beating in time with my heart as I walk down the middle of the deserted street toward the bridge. The streetlights are a dim, glowing orange in the dark, starless night. Heavy clouds have gathered above to block out the moon.

I walk, my shoes tapping the pavement with a calming rhythm. There's a loneliness in my chest and I know who it's for. I slip my phone out of my pocket and look at it. No missed calls.

I almost left Mercy a note, but I knew it wouldn't matter. It would fade. Seems that only a Seer can write about the Forgotten. Maybe Monroe will find a way to tell her about me. I try him at the clinic, but Rhonda won't put me through, even when I tell her it's an emergency. She takes a message. It could be hours before he gets it.

I'm ready to make my peace with the end. I have nothing left and I'm just happy to be almost done with this life. With no one remembering me, I feel like a ghost anyway.

There's only one regret. Not seeing Harlin one last time. If anything will follow me into the light, it's that.

I lower the phone to my side as I get to the middle of the bridge and look around. No one's here. I walk to the iron railing and peer over, the water below looking miles away. It's windy up here, and the thunder booms overhead, startling me.

I look at my phone again.

I love you, I type to Harlin, and hit Send. Even if he doesn't know who I am, at least I said what I needed to. At least I can give him that. I wait, but nothing comes back. He probably thinks it's a prank, if he got it at all.

"Loverboy not answering?"

I jump and look up to see Onika standing beside me, leaning her back against the railing. She's got on her makeup, her long blond hair flowing over one shoulder. Her black jacket is tied at the waist; her leather-gloved fingers tap on the steel.

"I told you I'm not going with you," I say. "I'm ready for the light." And I mean it. There's nothing here for me anymore.

Onika smiles and I can see how beautiful she must have been. Stunning. "You really proved yourself to me. I'm impressed. I bet Monroe said he was proud."

I freeze at her words, at how she knows things.

"You asked me once if I knew how to stop this. Do you still want to know?"

"Yes," I answer automatically. I know it's stupid, but I have to hear her out. I'm about to jump off a freaking bridge, I should know all of my options.

"Back when I was like you," she says. "Back when I was weak, a Shadow came to me. He was gorgeous. Sexy. He told me I didn't have to leave, and that if I stayed with him, I could keep my old life. But I'm not going to lie to you. It was a hard choice."

I watch her but I can't tell whether she's telling the truth or not. Monroe said not to trust her. I know I shouldn't trust her.

"You see," she continues. "I was in love. Me and Monroe Swift, we were pretty hot and heavy in those days. He must have told you how much he loved me, right?"

"He called you a beast."

Her delicate jaw tightens and I see a flash of anger behind her icy blue stare. Then she laughs as if I were only making a joke. "Tsk, tsk. The things he says now. Anyway, I nearly didn't go. I was at one of my compulsions—wait, what do you call it?"

"The Need."

"That's catchy. I was at one of my Needs when Rodney showed up, offered me eternal life. Power. The absence of pain and loss. All I had to do was stay out of the light."

"And now you're a hideous monster," I say. "Nice trade-off."

She narrows her eyes. "What a mouth on you. My mother would have called you a *telka*." Her Russian accent comes out thick. "Of course, from what I've seen, you're nothing at all like a prostitute. But to my mother any woman with a big mouth was a whore."

Her tone is venomous and I find myself backing against the railing to move away from her. The corner of her lip curves up. "I stayed for Monroe," she says before turning to put her hands on the railing, hopping up in a graceful, inhuman way. She doesn't need to hold on—she's balancing even in her high-heeled boots. "Come up here, Charlotte," she beckons, wagging her finger at me.

"Hell no."

"It's okay. You've seen it. You know you should."

The Need pushes me, almost like a shove in the back and I'm climbing, holding on to the cables next to me for support once I'm standing. The wind is blowing against me and I look back over my shoulder, terrified that I'll fall.

"Don't worry," Onika says nonchalantly. "I'll take care of you."

"I don't want your help!"

And suddenly there's a ripping in my chest, like a dagger has been stabbed through it. I groan and nearly lose my balance, but I hold on through the pain.

"I can make that stop," she says. "If you want, of course."

I look sideways at her. What happens if I say yes? Another pain assaults my back and I scream out. "Okay," I say. "Make it stop. I can't take it."

She closes her eyes and when she opens them, my body is filled with euphoria. Relief. The most incredible sense of calm I've ever had. I exhale, my head rolling to one side. It's like the best drug in the world.

"You can feel like this all the time, you know? I can make that happen."

I gaze lazily over to her, barely hearing the clap of thunder overhead. "How?" I murmur.

Just then, a flat splatter of rain lands on my glove as it holds the cable. I look toward it as another one falls.

"It's easy," Onika says. "Easier than this." I glance over to her, slowly coming back to my senses. She smiles. "You just step down off this railing and we'll leave. You and me."

"Sounds too easy," I say. There is a feeling in my gut, beneath this drug I'm on. It's like the Need is still there, only hidden. Like she's blocking it. "Is that what happened with your Shadow?" I ask. "You went off with him to become this?"

She laughs. "Oh, I killed that bastard long ago. He wasn't being straight with me, not like I am with you. And besides, I'm stronger than he ever was. And you, my dear, are like me."

"I'm not."

"Would you give it all up for Harlin? If you could still have a future with him, wouldn't you?"

"But how? If I'm immortal, don't you think he'd notice? Don't you think he'd notice my skin?"

Onika rolls her eyes. "Which is why we have powers. You show people whatever you want them to see. You can even control the weather." She laughs. "Personally I chose not to stick around, not when Monroe became adamant about sending me into the light. He was just using me. Like he's using you now."

"I won't do it," I say, desperately missing Harlin now that she's mentioned him. Now that it's almost over.

Onika grins. "I think you'll change your mind."

And then from the other side of the bridge I see two figures running toward me. I squint, but when they get closer, I feel my heart leap. Sarah and Mercy. "What? What's happening?"

"Maybe they don't want you to leave," Onika murmurs, and drops to a sitting position on the railing.

I'm gasping for air as they run up the empty bridge, stopping in front of me.

"Charlotte!" Mercy screams, her dark hair loose and wild around her face. "Get down from there. Oh, Jesus, help her." She looks up at the sky.

Sarah's eyes are wide as she stares at me. "Charlotte," she says cautiously. "Whatever it is, we'll get through it. Please, just don't jump."

They remember me. They do. All of the hurt I'd felt pours out of me. "This isn't real," I cry. "It can't be."

"Can't it?" Onika asks. "Don't they love you enough? Don't you love them enough?"

I take one hand to cover my eyes as I weep, not believing it's real, but not wanting it to be false, either.

"Sweetie"—I hear Mercy's voice—"come down, please. You're my little girl, don't leave me. Not like this."

"Charlotte Cassidy," Sarah cuts in. "If you jump now I'm going to be screwed up for life. You wouldn't want that on your conscience, would you?" I look at her and she holds out her hand to me. "Think of all the years of therapy," she adds.

My foot trembles as I reach it forward, ready to get down.

Rain starts to come down a little more and I feel it against the top of my head; a few drops land on my cheek.

"You walk away with me now," Onika says from next to me. "And you can stay on this earth. You can be stronger than you imagined. You will have everything."

I watch her. The rain is pelting her now, and slowly the tan begins to run, rivers of flesh melting off her face. She doesn't seem to notice, but the gray underneath is showing through.

Cracked, broken. Dead.

The sound of shoes slapping pavement breaks my thoughts. It's raining hard now, but I can see a shape running up the bridge toward us. The blond hair is unmistakable. Monroe.

There is a growl next to me, but when I look over Onika is gone. Still across from me, Mercy and Sarah stand, holding out their arms and calling to me.

"Charlotte!" Monroe yells over the pounding rain. "Are you okay, sweetheart?"

"No," I say. "I'm not."

Mercy beckons me to her. Sarah starts to cry and Mercy hugs her to her chest. They're both soaking wet. "Please," Mercy begs.

And then Monroe is in front of me, and I trust that he's real. I trust him. His hair is matted down and wet, and he's out of breath from running. "Wow," he says. "Your makeup is gone. It's just you now."

I look over to Mercy and Sarah, and I almost don't ask. But I know I have to, even though I can't stand to lose them again. "Monroe, do you see them?" My lip quivers as I gesture toward them.

Monroe's eyes widen, as if he knows what's happened. He glances around quickly. "There's no one else here," he whispers. "It's only us on the bridge."

I sway with sobs and as I look at Mercy and Sarah, at the people I love, they dissolve into rain and it's only Onika standing there. She sighs. "It could be real," she says. "I could make it happen. I mean, you wouldn't have *really* wanted them to see you like this, would you?"

"Don't believe anything Onika tells you," Monroe says, coming closer.

"She showed me Mercy and Sarah," I say with a whimper. "They were here."

"No." He shakes his head. "They weren't."

"Is it true that if I get down from here, they'll remember me?"

"It may be true, but you won't be you anymore, Charlotte. You'll be a monster." Monroe lowers his head, but his eyes still stare at me with determination. "It's your time to go. That's why I'm here. To witness. Don't step down from that railing."

"I know what he's going to say," I hear. I look over and Onika is next to me again, a sinister smile on her broken face. "You're going to love this part," she says, nodding her chin toward Monroe.

"Jump," he says. My heart stops.

"Jump," Onika mimics. Then she hops down from the railing and goes to him. Monroe can't see her. He's staring at me.

Onika walks, running her gloved finger over his chest as she walks behind him. "He really is still handsome," she says. She rubs his shoulders, even hugs him. "You have no idea," she calls over to me playfully, "how much he and I loved each other. Spent every second together." She walks in front of him, traces her finger across his lips. He stares through her, at me.

"Why don't you let him see you?" I ask her.

"Why should he?" she hisses, turning back to me. "He wanted me gone. He doesn't deserve to see me."

"Charlotte," Monroe calls. "Don't talk to her. Don't listen to her. Please, honey. You have to go before it's too late."

"'Honey'?" Onika turns to glare at him. "Isn't that endearing?"

"I don't want to be forgotten," I say to Monroe, ignoring Onika as she starts to circle him. "I want them to know how much I loved them."

Monroe nods. "No one can remember but a Seer. And I know it hurts. I'm so sorry. But if you step off that railing, you'll be chained to this earth, slowly rotting. You don't want that. Go into the light."

"Funny," Onika laughs. "And what if there's nothing there, Charlotte? What if he really just wants to get rid of you?"

But I think of Warren, and how I was with him in the end. How much I loved him, not as myself, but as the light. And I know there's something beyond me. And I know it's good.

Onika stomps back over toward me. "I'm getting tired of this game," she says, and waves her hand. "Let's go."

But I don't move. Instead I hold on to the cable and wait for the next pain to hit me. I close my eyes.

In the distance, above the sound of the rain, I hear something familiar. It's the sound of a motorcycle. I open my eyes and look down the bridge.

"Harlin called me," Monroe says. "He was looking for you."

"He didn't forget me?"

"Not yet."

I watch in anticipation as Harlin's bike comes up the high

point of the bridge and nearly spins out on the wet pavement as he sees me. His boots hit the concrete and he stops, his eyes wide underneath his helmet.

I'm balanced on the railing of a bridge, but I'm staring at him, overflowing with emotion.

He takes off his helmet, stumbling off his bike as he lays it on the ground next to him. He drops his helmet as he stares at me.

And I remember that I'm no longer hidden. My face is golden, all of me, really. I can't decide what he's seeing—if it's brilliant or horrible.

"He is handsome," I hear. Onika is sitting on the railing, picking at the leather of her gloves. The rain doesn't seem to touch her anymore. "It'd be a shame to lose him," she adds. "Lose that cute little apartment in the Pearl. The one with the painting studio."

I watch as Harlin comes closer to me. His boots are dragging on the ground, like he can't believe what he's seeing. "Charlotte?" he asks.

"Yeah," I nod. "It's me."

"Baby, what's happened to you?"

I shrug. "This is it, Harlin. This is my secret. I'm sorry."

"Sorry," he repeats. "My God, you're so beautiful." My sense of loss overwhelms me, and I sway, almost stepping down. But I fight it and hold on to the cable.

"They want me to go," I say. "They say I have to leave."

"Leave? No." He looks so devastated at the thought that I'm not sure I'm strong enough. I don't think I can leave him.

"To go where?" he asks, glancing between me and Monroe. Monroe shakes his head and wraps his arms tight around himself, like he can't handle this part.

"I'm not sure."

"I don't understand," Harlin says. "I don't understand what's going on. Come down from there, let's go. Maybe there's a doctor or someone who can help you."

"No!" Monroe shouts. "Do not get down, Charlotte. You'll be bound. You do what you're supposed to do."

"What?" Harlin spins around to glare at him. "Are you telling her to jump off the damn bridge? What have you done?"

In the distance sirens cut the sound of the rain. Monroe swears. "They're coming for you, Charlotte!" he yells. "They think you're trying to commit suicide. They'll pull you down."

"Good," Harlin says, and then turns back to me. "Whatever Monroe is telling you, don't listen, Charlotte. You don't have to go. You can stay with me."

"Wow," Onika says. "Maybe he's right. You should listen to him."

"Baby," Harlin continues, "I promised I'd take care of you. That first time you got on the back of my bike two years ago, I promised you that. I meant it then and I mean it now. I won't—"

The night stops. I hold up my hand to him. "You remember that bike ride?" I ask him. It can't be.

He nods. "Yeah."

"Do you remember our first kiss?" My heart is pounding beneath my jacket.

"In the hall. You were covered with green paint." He pauses, looking lost in the memory. "I ruined your white uniform shirt."

"You did." I burst out with a cry, but it's one of disbelief. I look past him to Monroe, who's standing there looking stunned.

"He's a Seer," he says. "That's why you're my last, Charlotte. Because now Harlin will take over." Monroe stumbles back, like he can't believe he's free. Free of the Forgotten.

"Another Seer," Onika says. "Didn't anticipate that one. Well." She slaps her hands together. "Glad we cleared that up. Now let's get out of here before the police show and you end up on the nine o'clock news."

"No. Leave me alone," I say to her.

She grins. "Say it again and I will."

The sirens are getting louder. When I look at Monroe, he smiles at me compassionately. "Jump, honey. It's okay to jump now."

Harlin tells him to shut up, and then holds his hand out to me, begging me to get down. He doesn't understand any of this yet, but I know that Monroe will teach him. Give him the journals.

But even with that, I still stand there, my heart breaking because I don't want to leave. I'm holding on to the cable, my body free of pain except for a faraway ache.

Then, the Need hits. Not the same way. Not like all the others. Over Onika's power a wind blows through me. It's love. It's calm. It's beyond me. My eyes set on Harlin's and when they do, his expression changes. "What is it?" he asks.

I put my glove between my teeth and pull it off before reaching my golden hand to him.

"No!" Monroe yells, his voice cracking with the force of it. Onika laughs next to me.

But when Harlin steps forward to take my hand, I only bend down to get closer to him. I stay on the railing. His face is near mine as he examines me, his expression amazed.

"Everyone will forget I existed," I whisper, taking my hand from his to touch his cheek. He closes his eyes and I feel all of my emotions, my love, fear, sadness, rush out of me and through him. He sees the Need. Everything I've done. And when I feel the last bit of me drain out, I let go. So relieved to be rid of it. So relieved to let him know.

My hand drops and he smiles through streaming tears. "You're an angel."

I shake my head. "I don't know what I am. I just know that I love you. And that I don't want to leave you."

The sky is lighting up with flashing blue and red and I see the police cars turn onto the bridge, heading toward us.

"It's time, Charlotte!" Monroe screams. "Go!"

But I stay, staring at Harlin. We watch each other, ignoring the rain, the sirens, my golden skin.

"Step down and no one will ever forget you," Onika says, sounding a million miles away. Just then I reach into my pocket and my fingers touch something smooth. I smile, pulling out the guardian angel that Harlin had given me.

I squeeze my eyes shut as I put it to my lips and kiss it. Then I hold it out for Harlin to take. "And now I'll watch over you," I say.

"Charlotte Cassidy," he whispers softly, taking the figurine from me. "I can promise one thing." His voice cracks. "I remember every word I've ever told you, every second I've ever spent with you. And I will never, ever forget you."

I don't hide the choke of tears that come out. "I'm going to miss you so much," I try to say. "I just love you so much."

"I will keep you forever, Charlotte. I will never let you go."

We look at each other one last second before he steps back from me, staring deep into my eyes with a love for me that only he can have. The love that tells me we are so much more than here and now. We are forever. We are complete.

Knowledge surges through me. Acceptance. The end. "Onika," I say, but don't bother looking at her.

"Yes, darling?"

"I think I understand the Need now. The purpose of the Forgotten."

"Really?" She laughs, the noise cutting through the sound of the rain. "Well then, by all means, educate me."

I look sideways at her. "The Forgotten are the only way the light can touch people. By being among them we can spread love and hope. We dodge the Shadows so that the light can shine."

"Wow, Charlotte. That's truly inspiring."

"But that's not all," I say. "I've realized something else."

"Which is?"

"That maybe I'm also here to stop you."

Onika's lips curve into a wicked grin. "That's almost sweet. But I'll be honest, love. You're not nearly strong enough to take me out."

I nod. "Not yet."

Onika's jaw tightens and she hops down from the railing, her boots making a loud clapping noise on the pavement. She begins to walk away, but then turns back to look at me. "I'll be seeing you on the flip side, Charlotte," she calls. "Enjoy the fall."

Suddenly I'm hit hard with a jolt of hot electricity. I scream until my throat burns.

My golden skin is tearing and little cracks of light are escaping right through my clothes. But as the light escapes, the burning is replaced with something else. Pure relief.

I find a way to lock eyes with Harlin again. And I smile at him, knowing he loves me. He'll remember me.

And then I close my eyes and let go of the cable, the feeling of tipping backward both exhilarating and powerless.

Wind is blowing past me and I open my eyes to look at the bridge above me. But I see only Harlin. And as I fall, he mouths, *I love you*.

The world around me is silent. And then there is an explosion of bright yellow light that extends to forever. A flow of emotion and heat pouring from me, illuminating the entire night sky. Illuminating the entire world. And in my last second, all I think is: It is so beautiful.

AFTER

i hear an echo as sound hums its way into my ears. It's a heavy
noise, reverberating as it gets louder. Louder. Louder—I'm
afraid my head will burst from the vibration, and finally my
eyes flutter open and it stops.

I see sky above me—blue and cloudless. Blinking quickly,
I try to get my bearings. Sensation returns to my fingers and I
dig in, feeling the grit of rock and sand beneath them.

In the distance, I hear wind in the trees. I try to swallow
but my mouth is dry. Sucking in a harsh breath, I start to sit
up, my body shaking. Vibrating. It feels . . . electric.

I bend my knees and rest my elbows on them as I look
around. I'm in a park of some sort: sandy hills with cacti surrounding me, a center fountain flowing on the other side of

a cement wall bordering it. Far off, I see cars crossing a huge bridge over a dried-up riverbed. A bridge?

Where am I?

Dizzy and confused, I stumble as I try to stand. I look down and my feet are bare.

Walking is odd and my legs feel off-balance, especially since the desert beneath them is hot and getting hotter. After a few yards I find a street, which is empty but for a few parked cars. I glance up at the sky again; it's so clear and sunny. I'm not sure why, but the light settles in my bones, makes me feel warm. Loved.

I start to move down the sidewalk toward the bridge, when a glint of light catches my eye from a car's side mirror. I glance over and look at myself in the passenger window.

I see a reflection, but it's not familiar. Suddenly, fear seizes me as I look between the bridge and myself. Feeling off. Feeling wrong.

Because I realize: I have no idea who I am.

ACKNOWLEDGMENTS

This book is dedicated to the memory of my grandmother, because without her it never would have been written. Gram, I miss you every day.

Next, I was lucky to end up with a dynamic duo supporting me. First, my amazing agent, Jim McCarthy, who believed in this book after reading only the first chapter. Jim, you changed my life. And next, my incredible editor, Donna Bray. I will be forever grateful for your guidance. It has been an honor to work with you. And thank you to all of the fantastic people at Balzer & Bray and HarperCollins.

I've written quite a few books over the past couple of years, and I have some friends who have suffered through every one of them with me, reading and commenting. I love you all: Trish Doller, Heather Hansen, Amanda K. Morgan, Bethany Griffin, Andrew Carmichael, Daisy Whitney, Hannah Moskowitz, and Rae Mariz. Plus all the incredible MUSERS who have let me vent and ask for advice.

I also want to thank Lisa Schroeder, Laini Taylor, L.K. Madigan, and all the other supportive local friends here in Portland. I bow to your amazing writing skills.

There were a few other readers and friends who helped me along the way: Kari Olson, Casey McCormick, Sarah Gundell, Mandy Hubbard, Josh Berk, and the Tenners. Also the SCBWI organization, especially Alice Pope. Special thanks to Lynny Waddell, Richard Raffule, and Dawn Goei. I wish I could name everyone, but this is already so long . . .

And finally, thank you to my family. Mom, I hope this book makes you proud. Natalie, I hope this book holds your attention. Alex, I hope you don't steal this book from the bookstore, and David and Jason, I hope this book gives us a reason to see each other again soon. Aunts, uncles, and cousins, I love you.

For my husband, Jesse, and my kids, Joseph and Sophia—this book is for us, our own little tribe. Without you, it means nothing. Thank you.